W9-CDK-959

NIGHTTIME EXPOSURES

The chair against the doorknob creaked. Someone was trying to get into the room.

Gunn was on his feet instantly. The night air chilled his naked body as he moved to the door and slipped the chair away. The door slid open and a shadow glided through the opening. Gunn grabbed the woman's arm and pulled her inside.

"I'm sorry," Deanne said, her voice startled. "I needed to see you." Then her lips twitched as she stared at Gunn at close range. "I certainly got to see *all* of you, didn't I?"

Gunn chuckled. "What's on your mind?"

"I don't think you should depend on my husband when he goes to look for horses tomorrow. You ought to go along."

"Is there anything else?" Gunn asked, his voice suddenly hoarse.

"There . . . there might be," she whispered. . . .

WHITE SQUAW
Zebra's Adult Western Series
by E.J. Hunter

#1: SIOUX WILDFIRE	(1205, $2.50)
#2: BOOMTOWN BUST	(1286, $2.50)
#3: VIRGIN TERRITORY	(1314, $2.50)
#4: HOT TEXAS TAIL	(1359, $2.50)
#5: BUCKSKIN BOMBSHELL	(1410, $2.50)
#6: DAKOTA SQUEEZE	(1479, $2.50)
#7: ABILENE TIGHT SPOT	(1562, $2.50)
#8: HORN OF PLENTY	(1649, $2.50)
#9: TWIN PEAKS–OR BUST	(1746, $2.50)

Available wherever paperbacks are sold, or order direct from the Publisher. Send cover price plus 50¢ per copy for mailing and handling to Zebra Books, Dept. 1852, 475 Park Avenue South, New York, N.Y. 10016. DO NOT SEND CASH.

#25

ZEBRA BOOKS
KENSINGTON PUBLISHING CORP.

ZEBRA BOOKS

are published by

Kensington Publishing Corp.
475 Park Avenue South
New York, NY 10016

Copyright © 1986 by Jory Sherman

All rights reserved. No part of this book may be reproduced in any form or by any means without the prior written consent of the Publisher, excepting brief quotes used in reviews.

First printing: June 1986

Printed in the United States of America

For Dan Killerman – a hellrider, and a hell of a writer.

Chapter One

The popping sounds of distant gunfire floated somewhere above the dawn, prodded Gunn to shift his tall frame. He was vaguely aware of the far-off noises and he tried to fight off the unwanted intrusion as he drifted upward through layers of sleep, struggling against the torpor of weariness. In this state of somnolence, his mind failed to register the importance of the gunshots, was unable to distinguish lines or shadows, could not define boundaries. He was dimly cognizant of a distant, urgent sound but his brain refused to fathom any meaning from the messages sent by his ears. Instead, he dreamed them into vague landscapes, and shaped them into meaningless explanations as if they were hail on a Conestoga's canvas top, or hard rain beating a brittle, disembodied drum roll against a tin roof.

The faint explosions sounded again.

Gunn rose from his slumber like a man drunk on Taos lightning, aroused before his sleep was through. He cocked his head, opened his eyes and tried to focus them on something tangible that might anchor his disarrayed thoughts. The sounds erupted again, a series of popping explosions like a string of Chinese firecrackers.

Those weren't the gunshots of hunters, they were the urgent, desperate gunshots of men fighting for their lives. And in this country, it could only mean Sioux.

Fully cognizant now, Gunn stood up quickly. His boots slipped in the ankle-deep mud, and he nearly fell again. His legs hurt from the cramped position he had slept in, tucked up under a small overhang. Neither the shelter of the overhang nor the poncho was adequate to the task of protecting him from the heavy spring rains of the night before, and he was soaked to the skin.

Gunn steadied himself, and reached down to rub the kinks out of his leg muscles. He tossed the slicker back from around his head, rolled it, mud and all, in one swift motion. He belched once. He was cold, sour-gutted and empty-bellied.

Esquire, the Tennessee Walker, stood head-down in the brush. The big sorrel's ears were laid flat against his head, and his coat was dark from the torrential rains. The horse lifted his head at Gunn's approach, but didn't flinch at the soggy blanket and saddle slung onto his wet back.

The whole world was wet, everything except his weapons. Gunn had wrapped his Winchester and pistol in a second poncho, wrapped that with a tarpaulin. In this country he took care of his horse and weapons first, himself last. The broken volleys of gunfire continued to echo through the rolling hills, bouncing from peak to valley to peak again, so that a man less experienced than Gunn might have no idea which way to go. Gunn had heard echoes of gunfire from Missionary Ridge to Dodge City to the Black Hills. He knew how to ride to the sound of battle, regardless of how distorted it might be.

Gunn swung into the saddle and turned Esquire north. Esquire broke into a ground-eating gallop, digging iron and throwing mud.

A man could run away in this country or he could join the fight. There were some who would have put as much distance between themselves and the gunfire as they could, but Gunn was not such a man.

Gunn's wife, Laurie, had been raped and murdered a few years ago, because there was no one around to help her when she needed it. Gunn had settled the score for his wife, but that was small compensation for the terrible loss he had felt. Then, as a promise to Laurie, he vowed never to run, always to help when he could, and to go into that permanent hole in the ground before he kowtowed to anybody about anything.

The big horse, startled by the need of an early-morning gallop, climbed the side of a hill with enormous, mud-flinging, gut-wrenching strides. He crested the hill, then half-sliding, half-running, plunged down the far side, across a draw, along the edge of another hump of soft slippery earth, passed some scrub trees, then to a rut of muddy wagon tracks that weren't there yesterday, through a grove of aspen and up another mound to a rocky outcropping. There, Esquire, with his nostrils flared and his sides heaving, skidded to a stop right on top of the shooting.

Ground-tying the sorrel behind a barn-sized boulder, Gunn scrambled up the last few feet to the summit, the Winchester .73 in hand, ready.

The gray-eyed man threw himself onto his belly in the mucky gravel at the very brink, wriggled up to the crest, then peered down the other side to see what was going on.

Five canvas-covered wagons stood axle-deep in the sloppy mud of the gully's bottom. Their half-moon formation frowned up at Gunn from the scant protection of a sparse stand of poplars.

Gunn sighed in disgust at whomever the damn fool was who was in charge of this small train. He had set the small caravan at the worst possible place. The wagons acted as a dam against the hellacious storm, catching the gully's mud and run-off with the wagon wheels. Then, to make matters worse, the horses were too far away from the camp to be protected. They were tied in a crude corral formed by running ropes from tree to tree and on the downhill side of a slope in the path of the runoff.

Several boulders lay a short distance outside the camp, and these afforded perfect vantage points for the attacking savages. The Indians had laid siege to the wagon train, and the reports of eight or ten rifles cracked as they spat death from behind the cover of the big rocks.

Gunn caught sight of a male body, naked to the waist, brilliant slashes of war paint on his face, as the Sioux threw orange blossoms of rifle fire toward the wagons.

The tall man stretched out on the ledge, swung his .73 into firing position and leveled the sights on the brave. The range was not difficult and Gunn's first shot hit the Brule in the shoulder, twisting him around. Over the gunfire and shouting Gunn heard the Indian's cry of pain, surprise. It was the last sound that he would make. Gunn's second shot caught the Indian right above the eyes, and blew off the top of his head.

A white man struggled with a brave in the mud near the end of the far wagon. They were fighting hand to hand, almost too close together for Gunn to have a target. Then the Indian knocked the white man down and, with a shout of victory, raised his war club. That gave Gunn the opening he needed. The Winchester barked and a small black hole appeared in the Indian's chest. He dropped his club, put his hand over his wound, and looked down in surprise as bright red blood spilled through his fingers. He fell to his knees, then pitched forward, face down, in the mud.

The corraled horses whinnied and stamped nervously, their eyes wide and white with fear from the noise of battle. Their nostrils flared at the stench of gunpowder and Indians.

At the near end of the line of wagons, a gray-haired man with suspenders looped over his longjohn-clad shoulders peered out from under a canvas flap.

"Get back," Gunn shouted at the man. He was too far away to be heard over the gunfire, and even if he could be heard, his warning would have been too late. Almost the instant the man appeared, a Sioux fired at the man from behind a nearby boulder.

The slug hit the gray-haired man squarely in the chest, the impact hurling him backward into the wagon. A woman screamed from inside the wagon where the gray-haired man was hit. A kid leaned out of the front of another wagon and fired several unaimed rounds toward the rocks.

Rifles flashed from under canvas covers, and this broadside was more effective. The fusillade knocked two of the Brules from under the brush; one somersaulted to the side with a shrill cry, the other ran onto his knees then plunged out of sight, face first into the weeds.

A Sioux bullet ripped through the canvas of a wagon. Another woman screamed as a man's body plummeted backward out of a wagon, made a sickening splash into the mud. The woman who had screamed jumped out of the wagon and slogged through the mud to reach her dying or dead husband. She grabbed hold of his mud-covered body and tried to pull him back, then fell across him as a bullet struck her chest. Her nightgown slowly changed from muddy white to brilliant red.

"Sonofabitch," Gunn muttered under his breath.

The most inexperienced tenderfoot could have done a better job of setting up the camp. The way the wagons were arranged, they were easy targets for an attack that could have come down from high ground in any direction. If the wagonmaster was still alive after this, Gunn intended to dress him down.

Behind the wagons—nearer Gunn's position—a brave flopped in the muddy grass. Beside him, rolling in agony, was a young white woman, her dress clearly stained by her own blood.

The defenders were firing from the wagons, but they were too frightened to be effective. Gunn could see seven Brules slinking closer for the kill. They would rise and make their final rush in seconds.

Gunn fired at the Indian nearest the wagons. The Brule rose straight up out of the brush, screaming a death-gurgle as a fountain of red spewed from his neck. He fell backward, his rifle tumbling through the air beside him.

Gunn swung his Winchester slightly, got a difficult, split-second shot at another attacker. This time he missed. With cold fury, the angry man laid down a heavy barrage of bullets, worked the rifle mechanism almost too quickly for accuracy.

A Brule—probably the leader—popped his head up and pointed toward Gunn's position. Gunn's Winchester held seven rounds, but he'd already lost count of how many shots he had fired. He reloaded quickly, figured he now had at least six more rounds in the chamber. He sent a couple of shots toward the leader, making him dive for cover.

Maybe the Sioux would think there was more than one man up on the ledge. They might think twice about continuing the attack.

Another Indian raised himself too high in the grass. Gunn's shot was quick and lethal. The Brule threw his hands high in a spasmodic death convulsion. The attackers seemed to make up their minds all at once. The gunfire stopped. Brush rattled as the raiding party retreated back up the slope the way they had come.

Gunn let out a long breath, figuring the fight was over. He rolled his head a bit to ease the tension in his neck muscles and caught sight of movement at the back of the most distant wagon. The flap of canvas whipped back and a slender, dark-haired girl—not more than 17 or 18—jumped to the ground and dashed toward the wounded woman writhing in the mud a few yards away.

"Get back, get back," Gunn shouted.

His warning was too late. An Indian had worked himself up to within a few feet of the wagons, and when he saw the girl come toward him, he jumped up to grab her. A second appeared from nowhere to join him. The girl saw them too late. She stopped and tried to get back to the wagons, but they caught her, and dragged her away, screaming and fighting.

Gunn aimed toward the dervish of activity where the girl was fighting her captors. Gunn didn't need much—just a hairline opening. Ironically, the girl's fighting was working against her at this point. If she would just go limp and let them drag her, he would have an open shot. As it was, every time he had one of her captors in sight, she would twist around and get in his way.

Then one of the Brules staggered off-balance from a well placed kick. The instant the brave was a few inches from the girl's side, Gunn's rifle spoke. The impact of the .30 caliber slug knocked the Indian over backward.

The second Brule hit the girl hard across the face. She went limp as he dragged her out of sight into the brush. Gunn didn't get a second shot.

Gunn cursed, then shinnied off his rock and grabbed Esquire's reins. He mounted in a single fluid movement, spurred around the outcropping, and headed down the slope at breakneck speed.

The settlers were still firing raggedly from the wagons as he galloped the big horse into the clearing and threw himself to the ground. He didn't see the girl or her captor and he ran into the creek gully looking for sign. The footprints were already filling with water telling him what he had feared. He was too late. The girl was gone.

He climbed out of the gully, and ran toward the wagons. A shot from high up the side of the depression nicked the mud a few inches away, indicating that, though the Indians had abandoned the idea of rushing the wagons, they hadn't quit the fight.

Gunn reached the protection of the wagons and crouched near a wheel. One by one the flaps on the wagons flew back. A boy jumped down and ran to the woman sprawled in the mud.

"Boy!" Gunn growled. "Get under cover!"

A hail of bullets drove the boy to cover.

The Indian that Gunn thought he had killed during the capture of the girl, chose that moment to stagger to his feet. Knife up, the wounded Brule charged the boy.

The two slender bodies entwined made a shot impossible. Gunn slogged through the mud and threw himself against the writhing pair, sending them both sprawling, and knocking them apart.

The brave sprang to his feet. Blood from a bullet smeared with the mud on his chest, but hadn't taken much of the strength out of him. The Indian charged Gunn, knife raised. Gunn saw then that the Indian was young, and inexperienced. Had the knife been low, his palm up, the Indian might have represented a threat. As it was, Gunn had no difficulty with him.

Gunn sidestepped and brought an elbow around to the Brule's Adam's apple. The knife went sprawling, and the young Indian went down hard.

Gunn looked around for cover, then realized that the Brules weren't firing down on them anymore. His eyes scanned the rim of the depression, caught the outline of a solitary figure. Gunn shaded his eyes with a hand and stared at the single remaining Indian. The Indian was too far away for Gunn to look into his eyes, or see the expression on his face. But the Indian raised his fist and shouted defiantly, then turned, and vanished down the other side of the hill.

The far-off sound of a cavalry bugle floated down to Gunn from the rim of the ravine. Help was coming. Where the hell were they half an hour ago?

People began scrambling out of the wagons then, weeping and staggering, taking stock of their dead and wounded. Gradually they surrounded Gunn, realized that he wasn't one of them, but had come of his own volition when he heard the firing.

"You saved our bacon!" a slender man cried, pounded Gunn on the back.

"Thank you, mister, thank you," a young woman said, weeping in fear or relief, or maybe both. She was clad only in her nightgown.

"June!" A rotund man yelled, looking around with eyes made wide by terror. "June? Where is she? Has anybody seen June?"

Gunn stared at the thickset man and at the blond, pretty wife at his side. "Was she a pretty girl?" he asked. "Dark hair? About seventeen or eighteen?"

"Yes! Yes, that's her! I'm Pat Bixby. She's our daughter."

"I'm sorry, Mr. Bixby," Gunn said. "I'm afraid the Brules got her. I saw them drag her off . . . I was too far away to stop it."

"No!" the woman screamed.

Bixby's eyes dilated. His knees weakened for a moment.

The young brave felled by Gunn's elbow to the Adam's apple groaned and tried to stagger to hands and knees.

"You! You heathen bastard! I'll kill you!" Bixby yelled.

Knife raised, he flung himself at the brave.

Chapter Two

Gunn moved in quickly. He hacked Bixby's arm with a stiffened right hand then wedged his shoulder between the settler and the Indian. Bixby staggered back a step. The Indian youth, his eyes white with fear and anger, started to rise to his feet.

Gunn backhanded him, and sent the Indian sprawling.

"Tie him up," he snapped at no one in particular.

Command set easily with Gunn, and even if he hadn't demonstrated his value by saving their lives, he would have expected his order to be followed. A couple of young men scurried forward to obey the tall stranger. The Indian found himself staring down the muzzle of Gunn's Colt .44, and he offered no resistance whatever, as the youths began to bind him. His shoulder throbbed from his wound, but he kept his face impassive, determined not to show pain to the white men.

"Let me kill him," Bixby choked. "Why did you stop me? They took my little girl! They've got June!"

"Don't be stupid," Gunn said coldly.

"She's our daughter! Our only child! Those savages . . ." The man was close to tears.

"You do want her back alive, don't you?" Gunn asked.

"Alive? What . . . what do you . . ."

"Do you mean there's a chance we can get her back alive?" the woman asked. Just in the few moments Gunn had known the Bixbys, he had already sized her up as the better stock of the two.

"Yeah, I think so," Gunn said. "You see, they went to great lengths to take her as a hostage. If they just wanted to kill her, they would have shot her when they had the chance. I don't think they intend to harm her. Not yet, anyway. And, if your husband doesn't do something stupid, we've got one of them. Maybe we can work out an exchange."

"He won't do anything stupid," the woman said.

Bixby stared up at the tall, gray-eyed man; the logic sank in.

"You saved our lives, mister," the woman went on. "Will you help us get June back?"

Gunn continued to appraise the beautiful, blond woman. She was tall, almost to his shoulder, and substantial. Her bare arms rippled with feline strength, her neck was smooth like polished alabaster. Her breasts resisted the restraining chemise, pushed against the cloth of the faded frock. Her flaxen hair hung loose across her shoulders. Hazel eyes flashed with determination and anger and with something else . . . electricity. She was no ordinary woman, and Gunn couldn't help but wonder how someone like Pat Bixby wound up with her.

"I don't know how much help I would be, Mrs. Bixby," Gunn finally said. "Anyway, here comes that troop we heard bugling. They're much more likely to be of help than I could."

The cavalry troop was commanded by Lieutenant Emory Slater, a bone-lank, narrow-eyed, bristle-backed man whose experience was greater than his rank. He had been caught on the frontier by reductions in the military, and a freeze on promotions. Lieutenant Slater had been a brevet lieutenant colonel during the Civil War. He was a contemporary of George Armstrong Custer. Custer reverted from major general to lieutenant colonel, Emory Slater from lieutenant colonel to first lieutenant. He'd served eleven years in grade. Eleven honorable years. Gunn knew him, knew him to be just, fair and by the book, resigned to the limbo he found himself in, but not embittered by it.

Slater rode in, set a few scouts on the rim above the death camp, and ordered the troops to dismount and search for bodies.

"If any of the Indians are alive," he ordered, "keep them that way. We want to ask some questions."

The lieutenant turned to Gunn and stroked his muttonchop whiskers.

"Hello, Gunn."

"Emory," Gunn replied. "Glad you dropped by."

Slater smiled. "Well, we didn't particularly have anything else to do." Slater looked at the way the wagons were set, at the distant corral for the horses, then he shook his head.

"I won't even insult you by asking if you're traveling with these people. My God, they were just asking for an ambush."

Gunn jerked his thumb over his shoulder. "Storm caught me last night. I was camped about half a mile away. I heard the shots and came at a gallop, but I got here a little late to do much good."

Slater nodded grimly, then looked about the camp. Around them, people were working over the wounded, mourning over the dead. The bodies of three men and a woman lay in the drying mud near the wagons. An old woman sat dazed on a barrel near a wagon while a slender boy wrapped torn linen around her forehead to cover the raw path of a nasty bullet crease.

Troopers dragged the dead bodies of Brules out of the brush.

"Who is the leader of this group?" Slater asked.

"Damned if I know," Gunn answered. "But I'd be inerested in that, myself."

"Boy," the army commander asked the boy who was tending to the wounded woman. "Who's in charge here?"

"Pat Bixby, he's the wagonmaster," the boy said, pointing to the heavyset man.

"You know him?" Slater asked Gunn.

"Met him for the first time five minutes ago," Gunn said. "He's shaken up some. Best go easy at first."

Pat Bixby stood with his stocky arms limp at his sides, a picture of desolation. In contrast to him, his wife was all over the camp, here seeing to a wound, there providing a comforting word, hiding her own pain and sorrow to be a help to the others.

"A man who'd take on the responsibility for a train and not know any more about setting up camp in a safer place than this, is criminally negligent. By God, if he were in the army he'd be courtmartialed," Slater said.

"His daughter's been taken hostage."

"I'm damned sorry to hear that, Gunn. But the crazy bastard brought it on himself."

"Yeah, I guess he did," Gunn agreed.

"Wait a minute," Slater said. "Bixby, you said. I never met him, but I heard of him. There were two of them, brothers, who came in with a train last fall, got caught by winter and were forced to stay over. One of the brothers stayed part of the winter, then lit out. His name was John, I think. He was a trader who'd done quite a bit of business with the Sioux, and a little scouting for the army. He scouted for Custer up at Fort Lincoln, which is why I never met him. Anyway, the way I heard it, he was supposed to have found gold in the Black Hills, somewhere. The one who stayed behind is a loudmouth, bragged all over the territory that he knew a place where you could pull up grass and find nuggets clinging to the roots."

"If the Indians heard the same story, that accounts for the attack today. They don't like anyone going into the Black Hills. That's sacred country for them."

"A fella like Bixby gets gold fever, it doesn't matter to him whether it's sacred country or not. Doesn't matter whether he's attacked or not, once they have the fever, nothing can stop them. I know, I've seen it too many times now," the lieutenant said. "I wish to hell they'd discover gold somewhere else . . . Arizona maybe . . . get these gold-hungry bastards off my back."

"If John Bixby traded with the Sioux, and scouted for the army, why isn't he in charge of this wagon train? Surely he'd do a better job than this man," Gunn said.

"The way I hear it, John didn't show this spring," Slater said. "He's dead, maybe. And after all his bragging, Pat Bixby decided to head on west anyway."

"The wonder is, he got anyone to come with him," Gunn said.

"Gold fever," Slater said. "It makes fools out of everybody."

Gunn watched as two troopers dragged in another painted body and tossed it with the others.

"So," Slater went on, "we don't have enough trouble, we have to rescue fools."

Gunn smiled. "You could be on garrison duty back east somewhere, parading every Saturday, polishing boots, brass and your C.O.'s behind. Would you like that?"

Slater chuckled, and shook his head. "No, I guess not."

Gunn's hooded eyes scanned the rim of the ravine. "You know the hostiles out here, Emory. Who do you think attacked?"

"Looked to me like it was some of Red Cloud's people. I got a view of the leader through my glass. Sure set his horse like Stone Legs."

Gunn's head jerked around. "Stone Legs?"

"Yes. You've heard of him?" Slater asked.

"I've heard of him. He's young, smart . . . ambitious. Some say he's crazy. He takes wild chances, but he's wily as a fox. He runs a pretty small band, but they're all first-class warriors, and they're always on the move, and they move fast."

Slater's smile was without a trace of humor. "Yeah, you've heard of him, all right."

"He's got the Bixby girl with him now. That may slow him down a little. Where do you think he'll head?"

"My best bet would be north," Slater said. "No telling how far."

"You got men in pursuit?"

"I split my men. Sent most of them after the ones we spotted."

"There weren't many of them," Gunn replied. "There couldn't have been more than a half-dozen left when Stone Legs lit out of here."

"That's how it looked to me."

"Will your men keep after them?"

Slater's mouth twisted into an expression of contempt. "Hot pursuit for an hour. That's the order. We've got a new colonel making all the decisions now. Before we came out here the only Indian he ever saw was carved of wood and standing in front of a cigar store. He's convinced that any chase longer than an hour will lead to an ambush."

"You won't catch Stone Legs in an hour."

"I know." Slater sighed, met Gunn's hard steel gaze.

"Which means," Gunn stated flatly, "that the girl is a goner."

The cavalry officer shook his head and shrugged. "There's no guarantee we could find her if we chased him for a week. She's not the first white woman to be taken, and more than a few of them never come back."

"Damnit, Emory, that's no reason to just give up," Gunn said angrily.

"I'm sorry, Gunn, there's nothing I can do about it," Slater said. He looked toward the wagons. "Well, I'll be taking your prisoner. The troops'll get these folks back to the fort."

The Bixby woman moved forward, her face pale, determined.

"Lieutenant, did I just hear you say you weren't going to try and find my daughter?"

"No, ma'am," Slater replied. "You didn't hear that. I've got troops out chasing them right now."

"For one hour, right?" she asked. "And if you don't catch them in one hour you quit?"

"Well, uh . . ."

"Tell her the truth, Emory. She's a strong woman,"

Gunn said.

"Yes, ma'am," Slater said. "If they don't catch up with them in one hour, they have orders to come back."

"Then you aren't getting the prisoner," she said.

"What?" Slater asked. He coughed in surprise. "See here, Miss, you can't keep an Indian prisoner. He's the property of the U.S. Army. I'll be taking him with me."

"No, you won't," she stated flatly. "The U.S. Army didn't catch him, and the U.S. Army can't have him."

"Mrs. Bixby, why on earth would you want to keep him?" Slater asked.

"Ask Mr. Gunn. That is your name, isn't it? Gunn?"

"Yes," Gunn said.

"Mr. Gunn, when my husband tried to kill the Indian boy, you stopped him. You said we might be able to work an exchange for my daughter."

"I know I said that," Gunn said. "But I was thinking for the army, not us."

"But if the army takes the Indian back to the fort, and makes no effort to exchange him, then we lose our chances to barter for June."

Gunn's eyes bored into hers. "Mrs. Bixby, I think you should know that the chance of an exchange would be mighty slim anyway."

"I know that, but what other chance do we have?" Her voice rose in desperation, nearly broke.

The lieutenant intervened. "See here, Mrs. Bixby. I'll take the prisoner. If Stone Legs makes contact . . ."

"Come on, Emory. You know the only possible way to make the trade would be to pursue Stone Legs north, make contact on his territory, then offer the kid for the girl."

"All right, Gunn, you want me to be honest, I will be. There's no way the army is going to take an Indian hostage into the Black Hills and barter with him."

"No, I guess not," Gunn said. "But I might." His voice softened.

"Oh, Mr. Gunn!" Mrs. Bixby said excitedly. She reached out and took his hands in hers. "Oh, thank you."

"Why would you want to do a fool thing like that?" Slater asked, knitting his brow.

"I saw the girl," Gunn said. "She was young, pretty, terrified. Hell, she hasn't even had a chance to live yet."

Slater's face twisted in thought. "The Indian boy might not be able to make the trip."

Gunn nodded his head toward the place where the Sioux was hog-tied and propped against a sapling. "Oh, I think he will. Look at him. His eyes are full of fire, there's no major wound. That slug only bounced off his collarbone. He isn't even bleeding."

"But that doesn't get to the heart of the real problem, Gunn. You know that I've got to take him back to the fort," Slater insisted.

"No!" Mrs. Bixby gasped.

"I have to, Mrs. Bixby. I have no choice."

"Emory, I just believe you're going to find some way around that little problem," Gunn said.

"You're serious aren't you? You're going to take this Sioux kid north and try to find Stone Legs?"

"It looks that way, Lieutenant."

"Gunn, I . . ."

"Lieutenant, you're wearing the same color I wore during the war. I don't want to fight the army," Gunn said.

"Are you saying you would?" Slater asked, his mouth tight.

"If I have to," he said flatly. A muscle quivered along his jawline.

Deanne Bixby watched the exchange between the two men, and shivered, chilled to her bones. This man, Gunn, was ready to fight if need be, even against the army. For the first time since dawn, she felt a surge of hope . . . that somehow this man might truly get June back.

Tension between the two men could have mounted, would have grown more serious perhaps, if Slater hadn't suddenly seen humor in it. He laughed.

"Hell, do what you want, Gunn," he said. "For all anybody knows, the Indian kid was with the party all the time. The colonel will never know the difference."

"Slater," Gunn's voice softened. "Thanks."

"Sergeant Collins!" Slater yelled.

"Yes, sir."

"Get the men mounted. We'll send a wagon back

for the Indian bodies."

"Yes, sir!" the sergeant replied.

Slater mounted his horse while, in the background, Sergeant Collins shouted mounting orders to the troop. Slater leaned forward on his animal and patted its neck. He looked at Gunn.

"Gunn, you put me through many more things like this, and I'll be putting in for that garrison duty back east you were talking about."

"Parades every Saturday," Gunn said.

"Yeah. Well, luck to you, friend," he said. He saluted, then rode to the front of the mounted column of troops.

"Troops, forward!" he shouted.

"Forward!" the sergeants shouted the supplementary commands.

"Ho!"

The cavalry rode off with their guidon, a swallow-tail Stars and Stripes, snapping in the breeze. Gunn watched them for a few moments, thankful that Slater had the right mixture of common sense and duty.

"You'll take the Indian north, then?" Mrs. Bixby asked Gunn, making sure she understood what had just happened.

Gunn's jaw tightened. "Yes."

"And try to find my daughter?" The woman was elated.

"Yes."

"Good. Then I may as well tell you now. My husband and I are going with you."

Gunn's slate eyes remained fixed on the handsome woman.

"No, I don't think so," he said. "I prefer to work alone."

"We're going with you," Mrs. Bixby insisted. "And that's that."

In the fierce light of determination in her eyes, Gunn saw that this was so.

Chapter Three

Gunn watched Deanne Bixby walk away, back and shoulders straight. The woman had been through hell this morning. Maybe, after the shock wore off, she would change her mind. Indian country was no place for a woman, even one as strong as this one. He vowed he would try and persuade her to seek army protection and leave the exchange of prisoners to him.

Deanne sat down wearily next to her husband. She looked him straight in the eye.

"Pat, Mr. Gunn is keeping the prisoner from the army," Deanne said.

"Why? Is he planning on setting him free? I should have known he had something in mind when he stopped me from killing that dirty little savage. He's probably one of them."

"Don't be silly," Deanne scolded. "If he really was one of them, do you think he would have helped us the way he did? Do you think he would have killed as many of them as he did?"

"Then why is he keeping the prisoner?"

"Because he's going to take him north to trade for

June. He's helping us, Pat."

"Oh," Pat said, chastised. "I guess we owe him our thanks."

"We certainly do," Deanne said. "But we're going to do more than just thank him. We're going with him."

"We're going with him? Why?"

"Pat, that's our daughter out there," Deanne said. "Don't you understand?"

"But wouldn't something like this be better handled by a man like, what did you say his name was? Gunn? That's dangerous territory up there. You saw what nearly happened to us this morning and we're just a couple of hours riding distance from the fort."

"Yes, but you were in charge of the wagon train. With Gunn leading us, I'm not afraid."

"I see," Bixby said, pouting with wounded feelings.

"Pat, you said it yourself, a man like Gunn is experienced in this sort of thing. And when it comes to getting our daughter back, I think you should be willing to swallow your pride and admit that Gunn is better for the job. Anyway, didn't you tell me that you wish you had an experienced scout to lead us into the Black Hills? Well, Gunn will be that scout."

Pat Bixby's bulging eyes lighted with sudden understanding. "Yes!" he said. "Yes, I see. This might work out just perfect. Gunn can lead us right to the gold."

"Gold? Pat, we're looking for June, not gold."

"Of course we are, dear," Pat said. "But once we get June back, we'll be in the Black Hills, just like you said."

"Come with me," Deanne said. "I want you to tell

Gunn that we're going with him. I don't want him to think it is merely my idea."

Any ideas Gunn may have had abut dissuading the Bixbys from going with him were dashed when the husband and wife confronted him a few moments later, insisting once again that they would go.

"I work better alone," Gunn said. "And this is certainly not a trip a woman can make."

Deanne Bixby's blue eyes snapped with anger. "I assure you, Mr. Gunn, that this woman can make it."

"We're sure to run into more storms, Mrs. Bixby. And hostiles. Late snow, maybe. Flooded rivers this time of year. Renegade whites that might take one look at you and start thinking of their own kidnap scheme. And there's something else you ought to know. The fella we're going after is an Indian named Stone Legs. A couple of years ago, the army raided Stone Legs's village, killed about eighty people. The only thing was, Stone Legs and most of the warriors were out on a hunt. About the only people killed were Indian women and children. Stone Legs has hated white people since then, and it makes no difference to him whether the white person is man, woman or child. He hates them all the same."

"What are you telling me, Mr. Gunn?"

"I'm saying that Stone Legs might not barter. Your daughter might be dead before we get to her."

"That's something I'm prepared to accept," Deanne said. "But it doesn't change anything. We're *going*!"

Gunn stared deep into the woman's cornflower-blue eyes. He found himself admiring Deanne Bixby.

She was strong and as full of fight as a wildcat. But despite that, she was definitely a woman.

Pat Bixby, not realizing that Deanne's quiet determination had nearly won Gunn over, grabbed the tall man's arm. Gunn jerked away from the fat man's grasp, and fixed him with a look.

"Don't ever do that again," said Gunn quietly.

Stung by Gunn's reaction, Bixby nevertheless plunged ahead. "Look here, Gunn," he stammered. "If you'll take us along with you, I'll make it worth your while. I've got money. I'll pay you . . . I'll pay you well."

"Don't insult me, Bixby. Do you think I'm doing this for money? I'll go because I want to go."

Bixby blanched. "I'm sorry. I just wanted . . ." he let the sentence drop.

Gunn looked at Deanne again. She was the strong one. He might back down Pat Bixby, not her. He let out the air in his lungs. After all, these people had a stake in their daughter's fate.

"All right," he said to Bixby, "the two of you can go. You and your wife. You can help watch after the prisoner."

"I'll get supplies from the wagon." Bixby's tone was eager. "We can start in an hour."

"No," Gunn snapped. "You'll take the wagon to Fort Laramie. Sell it and buy three good horses. Deep-chested, built to last on the trail. And a pack mule. Get supplies for at least a month, cold rations. We'll leave day after tomorrow, at dawn." The tall man's tone left no question about who was in charge.

Bixby's thick throat worked. He was not used to taking orders. "I'll do as you say."

"I know damned well you will."

Gunn walked over to the prisoner who was tied against the tree. He squatted and faced the boy. "You speak English?"

The Indian's face hardened, his eyes blazed with hatred. A muscle flickered in the tight, bronze jaw above the thin, compressed lips. "A little," he finally answered. "Do you speak Lakota?" he countered.

"Ay chay," Gunn answered, meaning that he didn't speak it well enough to be certain.

"Then we speak English," the boy said, proud of his superiority over the white man.

"What is your name?" Gunn grated.

"Charcoal Calf."

Gunn realized that the boy was feeling superior now, and he knew that he would have to show the boy who was in charge. He hauled the youth roughly to his feet, then solicitously looked at his wound, emphasizing with the contradictory action his own strength and authority.

"I may let you live," Gunn said. "If you'll help us."

Charcoal Calf eyed the rugged white man with even greater, more intense loathing.

"We're going after Stone Legs," Gunn explained. "I'm going to trade you."

"Do you think I am beads to be traded?" Charcoal Calf asked.

"Well now, I don't rightly know," Gunn said. "The question is, how good a warrior are you?"

"I am a good warrior," Charcoal Calf boasted proudly.

"Are you worth more to Stone Legs than a young girl?"

"Yes, I . . ." Charcoal Calf started, then he stopped in mid-sentence, realizing that, even in his own mind, Gunn had just regained superiority.

"Good, good," Gunn said. "I see now that we understand each other."

Charcoal Calf would slit the tall man's gullet if given a chance. Gunn knew that. To take the boy along as hostage was risky. But the youth was the only chance of getting June Bixby back alive.

It was a risk. One they'd all have to take.

It was early afternoon by the time Gunn paid the sheriff three dollars to house the Indian boy in one of the cells in his jail. After that, Gunn found a rooming house that rented a bath and bed for four bits. He intended to shake off the effect of spending the night in the rain.

The lean, rugged man soaked in the great, steaming wood tub for more than an hour. Then, with his skin burred clean from the soap and hot water, he dried off, lay on the bed. He knew it would be a long time before he saw another one. He shoved a chair under the doorknob, and still naked from his bath, crawled between the stiff, clean sheets. He was asleep within moments.

The room was still bright with afternoon light when Gunn fell asleep. When his eyes opened much later, the only light was from the soft, silver splash of moonlight. Something woke him. He waited, did not move.

The chair against the doorknob creaked. Someone was on the other side of the door, trying to get in.

Gunn was on his feet instantly. Like a stalking cat, he moved to the side of the door. He cocked his .44 and the metallic click of the sear and rotating cylinder was reassuring. The night air chilled his naked body, the rough boards grainy under his bare feet. His senses were alert, his body alive with intense readiness.

He could hear someone breathing on the other side of the door.

Slowly, without a whisper of sound, Gunn slipped the chair out from under the knob. A thin shaft of light shot in under the door. From somewhere in the night, a banjo twanged, and someone laughed, unaware of the tenseness in Gunn's room. Gunn waited.

The doorknob turned again and the door began to slide open, spilling in an ever-widening bar of golden light from the hall lantern.

Gunn watched the back of the door ease toward him.

A shadow filled the wide bar of light, gliding in through the opening, backlit by the lantern on the wall in the hall beyond.

"Damn!" Gunn whispered in surprise, let his breath escape in a rush, then grabbed the woman's arm and pulled her inside. He closed the door quickly behind her. The motion pulled her off-balance against him. For an instant the two were almost in an embrace.

"Oh!" Deanne Bixby gasped, almost falling. Her saucer-like eyes stared into Gunn's at close range.

Gunn slowly let the hammer back down on his .44. "What the hell are you doing here?"

Deanne wore a different costume. The dress was gray in the pale light, but it was soft, and clean smelling. There was a scent of flowers to the woman's skin. The woman stared at him, and as he became visible to her in the pale moonlight, her shock and fear was replaced by a sudden flitting of mirth around her expressive mouth.

"I'm sorry I startled you," she said, her voice trembling. "I didn't expect to find you like . . . like this."

Gunn shrugged off his nakedness. He muttered under his breath then backed into the shadows, and using a bedsheet restored some modesty, if not dignity, to the scene.

"You're mighty lucky I'm not the kind that shoots first, right through the door. Lady, you could've got yourself killed real easy."

Deanne placed flattened hands to her cheeks. The dim light from the window outlined the woman in its mist. She was substantial, shapely, beautiful. She was also trembling.

"I'm sorry," she said, her voice soft. "I needed to see you."

"Well, you picked one hell of a way to do it!"

Her lips twitched in unexpected bawdy humor. "I . . . I certainly got to see all of you, though, didn't I?"

Gunn chuckled. "I guess you did at that. So tell me, what's on your mind."

"I don't think you should depend on Pat for many things. When he goes tomorrow to look for horses, you really ought to go along."

"I know he can't lead a wagon train. But are you

telling me he doesn't even know horses?"

"He thinks he does. He thinks he knows a lot of things. Oh, if he was half as smart as he tells everyone he is . . ." She sighed, letting her heavy breath fill the moment. "I wouldn't be telling you all this . . . deriding my husband like this, if I didn't think it necessary. I want to find June, and I don't want Pat to do anything that will make that task more difficult."

"I'll go with him," Gunn told her.

"And you won't tell him I asked you to go?"

"I won't tell him."

"Thanks, Mr. Gunn."

The two stared at each other.

"Is there anything else?" Gunn asked, his voice suddenly hoarse.

"There . . . might be," she whispered.

Gunn watched her.

She moved across to the bed, sat beside him. Her thigh brushed his, burned through the sheet. Her bare arm nudged lightly against his naked, hairy chest.

"Gunn, I . . . I know you are a sensitive man. I could tell that when you were talking about my daughter being a captive of the Indians. A person who is sensitive, knows things. You know that I want you . . . don't you?"

"I know that you're married," Gunn said.

"I want you, Gunn," Deanne said again. "Please, don't turn me away. You don't know what it's like for me." Deanne made a little sobbing sound and offered up her mouth to him. He kissed lightly at first, then harder. She opened her lips, and almost of its own volition, Gunn's tongue darted into the wet, soft cavern of her mouth. Her hands fluttered over his arms and shoulders, squeezed, massaged. Her fingers teased along his chest, his nipples. The kiss deepened, heated.

Gunn knew he should have sent her away. The moment she came into his room, he had a gut feeling that she hadn't come to talk about horses. He should have sent her away, but he didn't. And he didn't want to now.

Her hands moved lower, brazenly, eagerly slipped beneath the sheet, caressed his thighs, then grasped his swelling manhood.

"Oh," she murmured, kneading his flesh into rising hardness.

Gunn began to work the buttons at her throat. She slipped one hand from beneath the sheet, to help unfasten the bodice. The pale light licked across her rounded flesh, the nipples pink, erect with desire.

Deanne slipped the garment from her body, then stood naked, washed silver in the soft light. Her flesh was smooth, her legs sinuous and strong, meeting at the luxurious golden bush. Gunn's eyes followed her flesh, past the soft, rounded belly to the uplifted breasts and erect nipples. She stood before him proudly, unashamed, letting him look at her, at her nakedness.

Gunn rose, moved to the door and replaced the chair under the knob, more firmly this time. He heard the bed creak behind him, and when he turned he saw Deanne stretched out, watching him, ready for him.

She held out her arms to him. "Come to me," she

whispered.

He went to her, and kissed her deeply, pressing his naked flesh against hers, feeling her hard little nipples burn into his chest. Her arms clung to him, her fingernails gently raked his back, his buttocks. One hand stole between his thighs to stroke his scrotum.

Gunn grazed lower with his kisses, along her jawline, her lobe, inserted his tongue into her ear, made her gasp and stiffen. He trailed his tongue down the long column of her throat to her shoulder, and down across the soft, smooth flesh of her breast to touch his tongue to the nipple. He took it between his teeth, gently, then began to suck.

"Oh, yes," Deanne murmured. "This is what I wanted. Oh, that feels so good."

Her hand between his leg grasped his cock, squeezed, worked up and down the shaft.

She kissed his forehead, his hair, while her body thrashed beneath his. She tried to get her legs under his body, to spread them.

"It's been so long, Gunn. So long." Her voice faded as the passion, the drive, filled the starved woman.

He could wait no longer. With a quick, smooth movement, Gunn was over her. She grabbed his swollen stalk, guided him into her throbbing gully. She was moist, slippery-ready, begging.

Gunn withheld his thrust for just an instant, to kiss her again. He pushed his tongue into her silken mouth, his manhood into her velvet cleft at the same moment. She sobbed and thrust her hips up as hard as she could. He buried himself into her long, hot pulsing tunnel.

She buffeted wildly, gyrated her hips, forced him to

go deep and fast, squeezing his cock with intense little muscle spasms.

Gunn rode her strongly, thrust deep, withdrew, thrust in to the hilt again. The woman beneath him cried out brokenly, crashed over the peak of the first orgasm, then moved on in quest of another. She muttered, moaned, tried to take him deeper. Lightning struck her again, and she shuddered with the pleasure of it.

Gunn was riding now.

Every stroke was faster, deeper. The lightning returned, and Deanne, writhing with pleasure, spread the fire from her body to Gunn's. Gunn felt the sweet-hot boiling of his own juices as he exploded into her, sliding through her hot-oil slickened tunnel to deposit his seed.

Afterward, they lay side by side for several moments without touching, without talking. Outside, the night life of Laramie continued, unaffected by what had happened here. Two men walked by on the sidewalk below, their boots making loud clumps on the board planks, their voices raised in conversation, intense only to them. A little farther up the street a piano had taken over for the twanging banjo, and there was a woman's shrill scream, then a burst of laughter. At the far end of town a dog barked, and, out on the prairie a coyote called for its mate.

Someone walked down the hall just outside Gunn's room, and Deanne, frightened, reached over and grabbed his hand. With her contact, the long quiet moment they had shared was broken, and Gunn sat up. He looked down at Deanne, at the silver light and dark shadows which played on her body. He touched her, gently.

"You'd best go now," he said quietly.

"I know," she agreed. She sighed and sat up, then, smiling, kissed Gunn lightly on the cheek. "Thank you," she said. "Thank you for saving our lives, thank you for going to look for June." She looked down at the floor, and Gunn could almost believe he was seeing her blush. "And thank you for being here, when I needed you most."

After she was gone, Gunn felt the familiar empty feeling return. It had been this way since Laurie had died. It was this way now.

Chapter Four

Pat Bixby stood at one end of the bar, bleary-eyed. There were two things at which he was expert; drinking red-eye whiskey, and talking. He was doing both.

He was bragging again. This time to a grizzled old prospector and a dancehall girl. Both members of his little audience looked about used up, the prospector wrinkled and dried by years of exposure to the sun, the girl dissipated by just as hard a life "on the line." The saloon was half-filled with a motley assortment of hunters, scouts, drifters, and sodbusters down on their luck. A piano, its veneer damaged during shipment out from St. Louis, sat at the back of the saloon. There, a black-eyed, thin-moustached musician cranked out songs which were often drowned out by the drone of conversation and the clink of glasses.

"You should have seen it," Bixby boasted, talking louder now, trying to draw a wider audience to his boasting. "A great band of hostile savages on all sides, more damn Indians than you ever saw before, come at us. I put my men in the wagons, the women too, them that would fight, and got ready for them. I was firing a Winchester and my old navy revolver as fast as my woman could load for me. Wham! I knocked down another one! Bam! Bam! Another one goes over backward with the front of his head gone. 'Course, it wasn't all one sided. No, sir, we was takin' hits, too. Micah Gibbons, you folks remember him, gray-headed guy with a big nose? Well, he got it. Jasper Marshall got hisself kilt too, 'n so did Mrs. Mayberry. 'Couple others, you wouldn't know . . . they joined us just as we was leavin', they'd only arrived from St. Louis. I tell you, it was one hell of a big fight, probably the biggest they's ever been."

"How'd you get away if they was all that many redskins?" the prospector wanted to know.

"Well now, I'll just tell you. The fact is, we got a little lucky. Now I ain't sayin' we wouldn't have won out anyway, but this here stranger come along and he was real handy to have around. Name of Gunn, I think. Any of you ever hear of him? Yes? Well, gents, he's a good one. I've stood shoulder to shoulder with many a good man in desperate battle, and Gunn's as good as any I ever seen. Anyway, what with Gunn and me both fetchin' our man just about ever shot, why, in a few minutes we had them savages on the run. They left bodies everywhere, plus they must of drug ten or twenty corpses along with them."

At a table in the middle of the saloon, Lucas Gorman, Maxwell Lee and Fred Wykoff sat drinking quietly. They were listening to Bixby now just as they had listened to him all winter. Maxwell Lee leaned over to Gorman, his round face red from heat and whiskey, and whispered, "He's gettin' a little carried off with hisself, ain't he? The army only brung back three, four dead Sioux."

Gorman held a finger to his lips. "Let the son of a bitch talk," he said. "When he gets to talkin' like this, he says too much. Maybe we'll get an idea where that gold is."

Bixby downed another shot and suddenly turned melancholy. His droopy, red eyes filled with tears.

"The only thing is, we lost the dearest thing in the world to us," he told his audience. "My own sweet, loving daughter, June. They hauled her off. Goddamn savages! They're animals . . . they're worse than animals!"

Bixby wiped his nose on his sleeve, then held his finger up. The tears stopped and his eyes narrowed. "But we got one of theirs. Yes, sir, we got one of theirs, and we're going after Stone Legs and his renegades. We're gonna trade with him. Our hostage for my little June. And woe be to the Indian that don't listen to us when we make the offer!"

He paused again, looked around, sighed heavily. "I wish my brother was here. I got a brother, John. A hunter. Tracker. Trader. Prospector. He can do anything. Some of you met him. Fine man, my brother."

Gorman had heard about John Bixby all winter. But the subject was not a dull one to the hardcase. He wanted to hear about John again, every word of it.

"John's spent years in the Black Hills. Knows them like the back of his hand. He knows where the gold is. That's why the Indians are callin' that land sacred, you know. Hell, the only thing sacred about it is the gold they got out there. They don't want the white man to know about their gold, so they make all this fuss about the Black Hills bein' sacred. Well, my brother found the gold. He found it, and he made a map of it." The braggart paused to down a half-shot, wiped his mouth with the back of his hand.

"I'm goin' to find my brother and join up with him, dig out the gold and come back rich . . . 'course after I find my daughter, that is. Yes, sir, when we come back, boys, we'll have my daughter again. And our pack mules will be straining to carry all the gold we've found!"

"Bixby," someone said. "You're as full of shit as a Christmas goose." The saloon erupted in laughter.

Lucas Gorman wasn't laughing. He signalled his two companions and the three eased out of the bar. Gorman, well over six feet tall, loomed like a bulky giant as they went to the door, and beyond into the chilly night. Maxwell Lee, fat, swaggering, with two guns belted around his middle, glowered through a bushy, smelly red beard. Lean and icy, Fred Wykoff surveyed the muddy street and its glistening puddles with the chill distaste that marked him as one who would kill in an instant for a glass of beer.

Gorman lit a cheroot and puffed dense clouds of smoke. "What do you think?" he asked.

"I think he's drunk," Wykoff said. "And like the fella said, full of shit."

"He is drunk," Gorman agreed, as he flicked the growing ash off the square-ended smoke. "But he ain't full of shit."

"Come on, Gorman, he's nothin' but a windbag. He don't know a goddamn thing about gold." Wykoff replied.

"Maybe he don't," Gorman mused. "But his brother might. His brother, John, is a mountain-wise old bastard, and there is gold out there. Who's to say ol' John didn't find it?"

"You think he really did find it?" Lee asked.

"I seen some of his nuggets," Gorman said. "Yeah, I think he found it."

Maxwell Lee spoke. "Then what do we do about it? I can't see letting that fat old windbag just waltz out there as pretty as you please and come back with a mule train full of gold. I want that gold!"

"Yeah, don't we all," Gorman said.

"The army," Wykoff pointed out, "says Red Cloud has broke the treaty."

"So what?" Gorman spat.

"I'll tell you so what. Red Cloud wants the Holy Road closed to settlers. The army's advisin' ever'one that it ain't safe out there." Wykoff explained.

"To hell with Red Cloud. And the army too, for that matter," Gorman growled.

"You got somethin' in mind, don't you, Gorman?" Lee asked. Lee chuckled. "Yes, sir, I can see it in your eyes. You got somethin' in mind."

"Only if we want the gold," Gorman teased.

"What? Well, hell yes we want the gold," Lee replied.

"I don't know, Wykoff ain't actin' like it."

"I want the gold," Wykoff said. "I want the gold. Now, what are you thinkin' on doin'?"

"We're going to let Bixby and his friends break the trail for us, while we just track along behind. When they find the gold, we'll steal it."

"Yeah, well there's one problem with that," Wykoff said. "We come through a hard winter. We ain't outfitted for travelin' like that. We ain't even got horses can make trail."

"You let me worry about that," Gorman said. "All I want to know is, are you with me?" Gorman turned from one man to the other.

"Yeah," Wykoff replied, his hawkish face lit in an evil grin. "I'm with you."

"Me too," Lee agreed.

The first peach dapples of dawn wiped across the still-gray sky when Jeremiah Heinrichs opened the slab door of his clapboard house and walked outside. He walked over to the rock he and his son called "pissing rock" and relieved himself, as he looked around at the new day.

Heinrichs, 30 and married, was an honest man from Ohio who had farmed his patch of grassland for just under a year. He had done well. The little house, tight against the wind, backed up against the south side of a grassy hillock. A few yards away stood a little barn, better-made than the house, and a corral.

Three horses stood in the corral, one for himself, one for his wife Patsy, who was pregnant, and one for his son, Jim, who was almost 10 now. Heinrichs had a milk cow, and a mule to pull his moldboard across the garden. In fact, he figured he had just about everything an honest man could want.

Heinrichs shook himself off, buttoned his trousers, then walked through the mud toward the barn. He slid the door back and stepped inside to get feed for the animals. A couple of chickens scattered into the outdoors, made a racket.

"Get on with you," Heinrichs called to them. He looked inside the barn, then gasped. A man was standing in the shadows of the barn. The man was lank with chill eyes.

"What do you want?" Heinrichs demanded. "What are you doing here, on my property?"

"No problem, old friend," the gaunt man said easily.

"No problem!" Heinrichs echoed. "Now listen, feller . . ."

Jeremiah Heinrichs got no further.

Lucas Gorman stepped out of the deeper shadow behind the farmer, a straight razor open in his hand. With a single violent movement, Gorman slashed the blade across Heinrichs' throat, opening a deep cut from ear to ear.

The farmer made a burbling sound and dropped to the dirt floor like a sack of feed.

Gorman stepped back quickly to avoid getting any of the fountaining blood on his good boots. "Like I said, friend, no problem," he said quietly. He looked over at Lee and Wykoff, who had been out of sight until now. "That takes care of the sodbuster," he said. "You know what to do."

Lee and Wykoff took off toward the house, running in a half-crouch.

Gorman waited in the dim stillness of the barn. First, there was a child-like shout, then a gunshot. A woman screamed, a long, frightened scream.

The woman screamed again and again. And again.

Gorman stood in the shadows for a long time,

listening to the woman as her voice grew hoarse, changed to animal-like yelps. Another gunshot came from inside the house. The screaming stopped.

Lee, then Wykoff, strolled off the porch toward the barn. Wykoff was buttoning his pants.

Gorman strode from the barn. "You shouldn't have killed her," he said. "I didn't get my turn."

The three murderers ransacked the house for provisions, then saddled Heinrichs' three farm horses. They tied the loaded mule on behind then set out for the hills. There, they would wait for Bixby, then follow him to the gold.

Behind them, the little farm looked peaceful, serene, beautiful even, in the first rays of sun.

In the barn the cow lowed for her morning milking.

The weather cleared, with a brisk wind blowing steadily out of the north. The absence of rain made the tracking fairly easy for Gunn. The tall man watched the trail for the unshod prints of Brule horses.

Deanne Bixby rode just behind Gunn, while Pat Bixby followed, leading the horse of the surly young brave, Charcoal Calf.

Deanne had avoided looking directly into Gunn's eyes since that night in his room. She was afraid to look at him, frightened that he might say or do something to give away their secret. Worse, she was afraid that she might do something to betray herself. Finally, she realized that the taciturn Gunn was going to do nothing to embarrass her, or cause her discomfort. As a result, she allowed her mind to slip back, to recall the pleasures of his bed, and such thoughts warmed and satisfied her during her long hours in the saddle.

The first day was satisfying to Deanne. She felt as if they were actually doing something to recover her daughter, and she was willing to brave any hardship, suffer any discomfort, if it would further their efforts. After a few days, however, the trailing began to wear on her. Wind and weather, along with meager rations, drew her face more taut. Oddly enough, it had the effect of giving her face more animation, making her even more beautiful.

In the close, bedroll camps there was no repetition of the single night of loving the two had shared. But Gunn often felt her eyes on him, and he knew what she was thinking. It sometimes stirred a tingling, twitching heat of his own, and he had to forcibly put the thought aside in order to do his job.

Pat Bixby noticed nothing.

Sign grew sharper along the trail. The small caravan was less than a half-day behind the Indians, moving carefully through rutted hill country of the kind that might have been designed for ambush.

Gunn made Charcoal Calf ride alongside him constantly now, not only so he could keep a close eye on the sullen brave, but also so he could watch him for subtle signs that might be a signal from Stone Legs. Indians, Gunn had learned, had an almost supernatural sense about these things.

Here, in the holy country of the Sioux, Charcoal Calf rode quieter than ever, his eyes fiercely vigilant, as if he looked for ghosts. The youth saw everything. Twice, a flash of recognition crossed the young boy's face, and each time it sent Gunn to the ground to examine signs that he might have overlooked.

Gunn learned, from the sign, that Stone Legs knew he was being followed. A skilled tracker himself, Stone Legs began making the trail more difficult for Gunn. He left false trails, and zigzagged back over solid rock, or lost his own tracks in the tramp of buffalo or wild horses or old trails. It was all Gunn could do to stay on the spoor.

"It won't be much longer," Pat Bixby said one night, as they all sat around the tiny campfire. The coals cast a red glow to his eyes. "We're close now, Gunn. I can smell it!"

"They're maybe six hours ahead," Gunn replied and turned the last of their fresh meat on the coals.

"I figure we'll have June back by day after tomorrow, then there's nothin' to keep me away from the gold. We're almost there, I tell you. I can smell gold like most men smell flowers."

"I'm glad you're willing to stop off and pick up your daughter," Gunn said sharply. "I mean, on your way to the gold."

"Of course I want my daughter," Bixby said. "That's the whole reason we're out here. Well, that and the gold."

"Yeah, that and the gold," Gunn said. "We'll be moving into the Black Hills tomorrow, into the heart of Sioux country. Stone Legs is no fool. If we start thinking gold instead of survival, we're going to end up spreadeagled over a firepit, begging to be shot. Anyway, what makes you think you could find the gold?"

Bixby chuckled excitedly. " 'Cause I got me a map,"

he said.

Gunn's head jerked up. "What?"

"A map. John gave me a map. I've got it." Bixby patted his vest pocket. "Right here. And we're headin' straight for where John says the gold is."

Gunn shook his head and frowned.

Bixby wouldn't have to look hard for trouble.

Trouble was bound to find him first.

Chapter Five

A few miles away, Lucas Gorman squatted beside a tiny, smokeless campfire with Maxwell Lee and Fred Wykoff. Gorman raised his voice in disagreement.

"We wait," he insisted, then ripped off a chunk of jerky with his ragged, tobacco-stained teeth.

"You heard the shootin'," Wykoff said. "They had to be fightin' off the Injuns. Hell, we would walk right in on them 'n they'd welcome us with open arms, thinkin' we'd be extra guns."

"They're goin' after gold. You really think they'd be welcomin' three more people?" Gorman asked. "Besides, I've heard of that fella Gunn. He's not one you want to tangle with."

"Gunn's got to get tired sometime. I say we hit 'em now, when he's not suspectin' anything," Wykoff insisted.

"So we hit him now, what have we gained? Bixby ain't found the gold yet."

Wykoff spat into the coals; the spittle made a sizzling sound. "Look, he took that Injun boy 'n split off today. Max and me followed him all afternoon. We seen him lookin' at that map, oh, maybe a dozen times or more."

"So what?" Gorman demanded.

"So, if you're worried about Gunn, we just wait until Bixby goes off on his own again. Then we kill him and take the map," Wykoff replied.

"But he ain't found the gold yet."

"So what if he ain't found the goddamn gold?" Wykoff snapped. "Don't you understand? We can take the map, find it our own selves. We don't need him."

"You seen the map?"

"Yes. I told you, me'n Max seen it today."

"No, I mean have you actually seen the map? The drawin' on it?"

"How the hell could we see it from where we was?"

"That's what I'm getting at," Gorman said. "Even if it is a map, that ain't sayin' we can read it. He might have it wrote down in a way that only he can read it. That's why I'm for waitin'. When Bixby actually finds the right spot and I can see the gold in his hands, that's when we hit. Let him find it, let him dig it out."

Wykoff looked at Gorman out of the corner of his eye, half-convinced. He tossed a pebble from hand to hand with impatience.

"Besides, look at it this way," Gorman added. "The Brules don't even know we're back here. They're lookin' at Gunn and he's lookin' at them. Nobody's giving us any trouble. If we join up with Gunn, them Injuns gonna take notice of us. So why ask for trouble?"

Maxwell Lee stirred the fire. He finally spoke. "Hell, that makes sense to me, Fred," he said to

Wykoff.

"Yeah, well there's somethin' else I'm wantin' in the bargain," Wykoff growled. "I want that woman. I want her bad."

"Think about this," Gorman suggested. "S'posin' they catch Stone Legs in some kind of a trap, git Bixby's daughter. You remember seein' her aroun' the fort this winter. Young, saucy, dark hair."

Wykoff stared at Gorman with dull, bloodshot eyes. "So?"

"Well, if that happens," Gorman explained, "we don't just get one woman . . . we get two. Two, and the gold."

Wykoff blinked, stared at the dying coals for a moment.

"Yeah," he said. He smiled crookedly. "Yeah, now that does make sense."

"The time will come," Gorman added.

"Soon, you think?"

"Yeah, Fred. I think real soon, now."

The sun was only a burnished half disc above the horizon, and the light was soft and the air was cool as Gunn set about breaking camp and saddling horses. Bixby already let it be known that he would be taking Charcoal Calf with him again, today. That meant that the opportunity for Charcoal Calf to escape was much greater than it was when all of them were together. And, even if he didn't escape, they were an easier target for Stone Legs when they were split up.

Nevertheless, he had no intention of trying to force them all to stay together. The truth is, he trailed better without Bixby's constant gab. The woman was easier to trail with, she was strong, sensible, and determined enough to get her daughter back that he had no problems with her.

"You figure Stone Legs will attack again today?" Bixby asked as the small party left camp.

"I don't look for trouble," Gunn said.

"What can he do?" Bixby asked, talking to himself. "He's only got four or five braves left."

"Numbers don't mean much."

"I don't know. I think he's all used up."

"Look, Bixby, you believe what you want. Stone Legs is on home ground. I wouldn't sell him short, was I you."

"You're talkin' like you're ready to quit. You ain't thinkin' on givin' up, are you?"

Gunn glared at Bixby with a stare that could stun a horse.

Bixby paled. "I'm sorry," he apologized quickly, realizing he had nearly overstepped his bounds. "I guess I got a big mouth."

Gunn said nothing. He urged Esquire on ahead, gaining a few paces on the fat man.

The morning sun climbed higher, brighter in the eastern sky as the horses moved along in single file, their riders silent.

Every few minutes Bixby would pull out the map and study it, the chill spring wind causing it to flutter over his knees and saddlehorn.

"I'm going over this way," he shouted, pointing toward a distant break in the rolling hills.

"I don't suppose it matters to you that the trail leads the other way," Gunn yelled back into the breeze.

"That don't mean nothin'. The trail's cold. They're too far ahead. I'll take the boy with me."

"I thought you might," Gunn said. Bixby was nerve-wracking even when he was quiet. If he rattled that damned map once more, every Sioux within 20 miles would hear it.

"The river's just ahead," Bixby replied with poorly controlled excitement. "It can't be far. Today might be the day I find it."

"The river?" Gunn asked.

"No," Bixby laughed, "the gold!"

"Pat," Deanne pleaded.

"Let him go," Gunn said, a brusqueness to his tone.

Bixby looped a lead rope roughly around Charcoal Calf's neck, made the young brave glare with outrage. Bixby yanked the coil taut, creased the boy's neck. Any attempt to get away—even a misstep by his horse—might break Charcoal Calf's neck.

Gunn rode up hard, stood Esquire in Bixby's path.

"That's not a dog on leash, Bixby. You tie him where he can breathe or I'll take that rope and drag brush with you."

"Hell, I just wanted to . . ."

"Don't try my patience any more. You get that rope off his neck, pronto, or tangle." Gunn had come to help a young girl, not quarrel with her father. If Bixby did one more thing off-center . . .

"All right," said Bixby, grudgingly. He loosened the rope, looped it around Charcoal Calf's chest, led the Indian away. The two riders wound their way down a long, wooded arroyo, then disappeared beyond the trees.

"He's such a fool," Deanne sighed, her eyes focused on the empty gully. "Sometimes . . . sometimes, I just hate him!" The anger in her voice was genuine.

"If you feel that way, why do you stay with him?" Gunn queried.

Deanne's angry eyes burned into Gunn's. "What does a woman alone on the frontier do? Work in a dance hall? Let drunken cowboys have their way with her for a half-dollar?"

"You're a resourceful woman," Gunn said.

"A woman doesn't have a chance out here alone."

"A lot of men don't either," Gunn added. "But that's no excuse not to try."

"Are you telling me I should leave him?" Deanne asked, a measure of hope creeping into her voice.

"No," Gunn said. "I'm telling you to do what you want to do, without making excuses."

"It's not as easy as all that, Gunn," Deanne said. "I wish it was, but it isn't."

After that, the two rode in silence, Gunn often leaning far to the side in the saddle to read the signs in the dirt and rock. They were headed almost due north now.

The day wore on, warming, a hot sun breaking through wispy, fast-moving clouds. The sign Gunn read became confusing. The trail of more unshod ponies crossed those of Stone Legs and his band, mixed with them for a while, then went away again.

"Stone Legs might have got some help here," Gunn said as he pointed to the tracks.

"Or maybe not?" Deanne asked, worry in her tone.

"Or maybe not," he conceded.

"They split up, you say?"

"Yes, some went west."

"Pat went west, somewhere," she remarked.

"Yes."

They trailed until sunset, then, with a western bank of clouds glowing gold and red in the dying sun, they stopped and made camp against the face of a sheer granite cliff. A cave, its mouth grown over with brush, cut back into the rock. Gunn led the animals a few yards away, sheltered them under an overhang of rock, hobbled them securely. They wouldn't wander far in the pitch dark.

The clouds were belly-lit now, still gleaming underneath, but purple above. They began to gather in great, billowing puffs, and, on the westerly breeze, there was a smell of rain. Gunn watched until the last vestige of light had died, and darkness had shrouded the land. He saw nothing, no one.

In the cave, Gunn did not set a fire, but dug out a nub of a candle. Deanne dropped wearily on the clean, rocky floor, then began brushing her long, silken hair as she did every night.

Gunn crept back outside, made sure the candle light couldn't be seen from any angle, then went in again.

"Pat won't be able to find us tonight," Deanne said quietly.

Gunn handed her some jerky and parched corn. "I know."

"He might have gotten himself killed."

The tall man kept silent.

Deanne laid the brush aside and hugged herself, trembling. "I'm afraid," she murmured.

"You?" He replied. "I find that hard to believe."

Her eyes met his. "I'm just a woman, Gunn."

"Ah," he let out a long breath. "I know you're a woman."

Her face softened. "You've thought about that night back in Laramie?"

"Yes."

"Often?"

"Often enough."

Deanne slid back against the rock wall of the cave. She patted the ground beside her. "Gunn," she breathed softly.

"Might not be a good idea. Someone . . ."

"You just said no one can find us."

"Yeah, maybe, maybe not." He got up and moved to her side.

The closeness of her stirred him. She smelled of woman; of sweat and the musk of a woman in season. She leaned against him, her breasts pressing insistently against his arm.

Her face moved close to his, her lips pressed against his own. She flicked her tongue hotly into his mouth, explored, licked, sucked.

Gunn crushed her against him, fired by his need for her.

"Wait," she panted, broke away.

He tried to pull her close.

She stood, began tearing off her clothes. In the golden wink of the candle, she was a study in light and shadow, one nipple glaringly revealed, the other seductively concealed. Her dress was gone, flung aside on the earthen floor.

"You too," she whispered. "Hurry!"

Gunn stripped out of his clothes and felt the massage of cool cave air against his skin. He saw in Deanne's eyes the reflection of the flame of the candle. The burning flame blended with her natural light so that it looked as if it had been kindled by the heat of her desire. He reached for her, but she stepped back.

"What—?" he began.

She went onto her knees in front of him, then pressed her hot palms against his hips.

Deanne leaned over him between his spread legs, took his cock in her long, supple fingers. "So beautiful," she murmured. She squeezed his manhood gently.

Gunn groaned. A silver droplet appeared on the slit of his swollen shaft.

"Oh, my," Deanne whispered. Her tongue darted out, sending a jolt of pleasure through him. The drop disappeared.

Gunn groaned again.

"You taste good," she told him. "I want to taste more."

Deanne took a deep breath, then bent over him, taking his cock into her mouth. She moved her lips down the shaft, feeling the soft crown against her palate, flicking her tongue against the slit, tasting the fluids that seeped out warm and salty. She moved her mouth back to the head, then down, as far down on the shaft as she could, sliding him in and out of her mouth. Her loins churned with heat, her juices boiled, bubbled through her bush.

After a few moments of this, she released his engorged cock and began to make her way up his belly, raining tiny kisses across his lean body.

He grasped her in his arms, rolled her over, felt her juices which had spilled over, He had grown larger in her eager mouth, his desire more urgent.

Quickly he lowered his body onto her soft, resilient frame. She spread her legs for him, her pink vulva opening in anticipation, begging for the ultimate invasion. He slipped his cock into the oiled, velvet sheath.

Deanne gasped as she felt him plunge deep inside her. She thrashed against him, making little sobbing sounds, as he withdrew, slid in, then withdrew again. The muscles of her love tunnel squeezed, massaged his shaft, milked him for his seed.

The two locked together, plunging, rising. The wet sound of flesh against oiled flesh echoed through the shallow cave.

Deanne stiffened, moaned as the first wave of orgasm swept over her body. Gunn continued unabated, pounding deep into her welcoming cleft. Her moans grew in intensity, becoming enraptured cries which filled the cave as wave upon wave of pleasure consumed her.

Gunn felt himself sliding forward, and, knowing that Deanne had already orgasmed he made no effort to hold back but rode with it, melting and pouring out of the end of his cock. The first enormous gush traveled the length of his cock and exploded into her velvet smoothness. She felt him, and gasped with the final pleasure, staying with him as his seed boiled out of his body.

Finally spent, he fell from her, breathing hard.

Deanne snuggled up to the length of his body and kissed him gently, then passionately, on the mouth. Her fingernails bit into his flesh as she pressed against his body.

"Thank you," she murmured. "That was wonderful."

It was late when they finally curled in each other's arms, still naked, to fall asleep under the warmth of a buffalo robe.

Gunn awakened once during the night, and he put his hand across to feel her lying there with him. He let his hand rest lightly across her pelvis, feeling the different textures of smooth skin, the sharpness of the bone beneath, and the coarse bush of her pubic hair.

He pulled his hand away. It wasn't good to get too attached to such sensations. That was getting too close to the soul . . . the inner man that he had shared with no one since Laurie.

Chapter Six

Gunn looked at the slate sky, the low-hanging clouds, gray with morning light. The rain he had expected the night before hadn't materialized as yet, but the weather was still threatening. Bixby and Charcoal Calf didn't show during the night, and were nowhere in sight this morning.

"I guess we'll have to go find them," Gunn said. "They must be lost."

Deanne drew herself up to the tall man, kissed him deeply.

"Be careful," Gunn growled.

"I will," she assured him. "I just wanted something to remind me of last night."

"Right now," Gunn told her, "we have to move on."

"I know," she smiled. "And don't worry. Our little secret is safe with me."

Gunn looked at her for a moment. "Deanne, I don't want you to get the wrong impression about things . . . to see something that isn't there, to hope for something that can't be," he said.

Deanne looked at Gunn for a moment, and her eyes clouded, misted.

"You . . . you aren't talking about June, are you?" she said. "Because you know I'm already prepared for whatever happens there."

"No. I'm not talking about June," Gunn answered.

"Gunn, didn't you . . . that is, I thought you felt the way I did. I thought you wanted me as much as I wanted you," Deanne said.

"I wanted you," Gunn said. "When this is over, I'll drift on, like always. I ride a lone trail."

"I'm sorry," Deanne said quietly. "I guess I've been making a fool of myself."

"No, you haven't," Gunn said. Gunn put his fingers on her cheeks. "Deanne, if things were different . . . if I could live the life of an ordinary man, I don't think I could find any woman more desirable than you. And I'd take you away from Pat however I had to do it. I hope you can understand, and not be hurt."

Deanne's eyes flooded with tears, but she smiled through them.

"I'm not a fresh young farm girl, Gunn. I'm a grown woman, and I like to think I'm a strong woman. I guess I understand. I'll just be grateful for what we've got, while we've got it."

Gunn smiled at her. "Deanne, you're one hell of a woman," he said. He sighed, and looked around. "Now, I guess we'd better see what we can do about finding your husband."

Gunn went back over the ground they'd covered the day before, a little angry at the delay. He soon picked up the trail of Bixby and the boy. Their tracks headed deeper into the hills, followed shallow canyon pathways.

The tracks halted beside a meandering stream.

There was ample sign that Bixby had stopped here to pan for gold. Gunn saw muddy footprints and little piles of silt on the shoreline. The two had spent several hours by the creek. Gunn found an empty whiskey bottle, a few quids of chewed tobacco, a smell of urine on a bush.

From there, the tracks led northward, climbing into slightly higher terrain. Gunn signaled Deanne to follow.

"He didn't even try to turn back and find us," she puzzled. The tracks were so obvious that even she could read them.

"These sign were made about mid-day. He might have doubled back later, come through a different valley."

"You mean we might be tracking in a big circle?" she asked.

"We might," Gunn replied. He took a drink of water, corked his canteen, then hooked it back over the pommel.

"We might end up going right back where we started?"

"Could be, if that's where the trail leads." Gunn agreed.

"Damn him!" Deanne swore. "Has he completely forgotten what we're here for?"

"I don't think he's forgotten what he's here for," Gunn said, a faint sarcasm latched to his tone.

"But our daughter is up there somewhere, being held by savages! God only knows what they're doing to her!"

"He doesn't seem much bothered," Gunn said drily.

"And all because Jack left him that stupid map!"

"Jack?"

"Pat's brother, John Bixby. He—he lives out here, somewhere. Has for years. I wish he would show up. He could help us find June. He'd certainly be more help than Pat."

"Maybe. Odd the Sioux would let a white man living in the Paha Sapa keep his scalp. Likely he's managed to stay out of their way. Man like that wouldn't want to make much noise or come out open against the Sioux."

Deanne's eyes filled quickly with tears, and she gasped. Gunn was surprised by her reaction, and he walked over to her.

"I'm sorry, Deanne," he said. "I shouldn't have spoken like that. I didn't realize you were so close to your brother-in-law."

Deanne faced Gunn, a fiery sadness in her eyes. She brushed her hair back from her face. "We were much closer than you think," she said quietly.

"What do you mean?" Gunn asked, puzzled by the turn of events.

"June isn't Pat's daughter," Deanne said. "She's Jack's."

"What?"

"She's Jack's. Jack's and mine."

Gunn stared at her for an intense minute, digesting what she had said to him. He let out a long, slow breath.

"Does Pat know?" he asked.

"No. We were unable to have a child. We tried, but there was something . . . something wrong with Pat. He was infertile for some reason. In the early days, he took it out on me. Blamed me for the children we couldn't have, bragged about how many children he had whelped with other women . . . loose women." Deanne wiped her eyes. "I believed him, I was young, inexperienced, I didn't know any better.

"Then one day Jack came to visit. It was the first time I'd ever seen him." Deanne smiled. "Oh, he was so handsome, and romantic. He'd been a scout for the army . . . he was thin, hard, strong. I fell in love with him . . . or at least, I fancied that I did." Deanne sniffed, and smiled through her tears. "Much like I have with you, I suppose. Anyway, when Pat got drunk and ugly one night, and stormed out of the house, I . . . I was fair game for Jack. I won't say he seduced an innocent young girl, Gunn. I confess that I egged him on. Anyway, when I found out that Jack had made me pregnant, I pretended it was Pat's. He was as eager to accept the baby as his own as I was to hide the truth. He told everyone that all I needed was a good man to make me pregnant, and he was that man."

"How did he treat the girl?" Gunn asked.

"He loved her. He loved her from the time she was born, and he was always good to her."

"And his brother?"

"Jack?" Deanne sniffed, and Gunn handed her his handkerchief. "Why, you would've thought the sun rose and set on Jack," she said. "Pat was always close to him, bragged about him as if Jack's exploits were his own. He never showed the slightest sign of jealousy."

"And what about you and Jack?"

"Never again," Deanne said. "And until that night back in Laramie with you, I was never unfaithful to

Pat again. You know, I really believe that's why Jack came out here to the Black Hills to search for gold. I think he couldn't stand it, being around me and Pat, wanting me . . ." Deanne's voice trailed off.

Gunn rolled a smoke and wondered what kind of mess he had gotten himself into. He thought briefly of saying to hell with the whole thing and turning back. But June Bixby was out there somewhere. None of this was her doing; she was an innocent victim of circumstances. And she had gotten captured in the first place, because she had risked her life trying to help someone else. Gunn remembered the brief glimpse he had of her as the Brule dragged her off. Slender, dark, young, innocent, terrified. No, he would stay.

Deanne watched Gunn, studied his face until the cigarette was smoked down. Finally, he tossed the cigarette down, ground it under his boot heel.

"Let's get moving," he said. "See if we can catch up with them."

The pair rode for an hour. The man scanned the ground, then the horizon, hunting, searching for sign. Then he found tracks that were new to him.

"What the hell?" he barked.

"What is it? Gunn, what have you seen?" Deanne asked, frightened by his sudden outburst.

The tracks Gunn was looking at were those of shod horses. White man's horses. Three sets of hoofprints in light, loamy soil on a hillside where most trackers would have missed them. They weren't Indian ponies, and they weren't the horses of Bixby or Charcoal Calf. The tracks were separate, curving westerly, heading toward the gap in the mountain ahead, a gap that marked a river gorge.

The prints were fresher, made earlier today.

They had come up from the south, skirted Gunn's route, by the look of it, then moved ahead of him to follow Pat Bixby and the boy.

"Son of a bitch!" Gunn said.

"Gunn, what is it?" Deanne asked again.

"We've got company," Gunn said. "White men. Come on, we've got to ride hard now."

In the river gorge, mist hung like gauze between rising hills.

The river, winding north to southeast, wended through scraggly woods, the rolling prairie floor of the valley, and into the narrower gorge where it broke into white water over the rocks and outcroppings.

A rock formation jutted fully one hundred feet above Pat Bixby.

The towering shape looked like a chess piece; a rook.

Bixby held his brother's map in shaking hands.

The map showed the river course, crudely but accurately. And there was an X beside the word: Castle.

The designation had troubled Bixby until now. Now he understood. When he and his brother played chess, Jack had always called the rook a castle.

"This is it!" Bixby cried in a shaky voice. "You hear me, you stinking savage? This is it! This is the place my brother drew on the map! I knew we shouldn't go back to camp last night. I've found it!"

Bixby stared at the map again. Eagerly he looked

up, spied other landmarks—a low round hill off to the west, a crooked peak, a little creek feeding into the river.

Below, three or four miles distant, a jumble of rocks from an ancient landslide lay hot in the sun. Everything checked out, just like it was on the map.

The fat man referred to the map again, saw the circle with an X through it; the place that marked the location of the gold.

Bixby pointed, shaking like an old man with the ague. "It's there. Right down there! Under that slide!"

The man grabbed the lead halter of the brave's horse, then started down the long, rocky slope at a dangerous, frantic speed.

Lucas Gorman lowered his spyglass, slammed it shut, and put it back in the saddlebag. He turned to his companions, a crooked grin on his ruddy, stubbled face.

"He's found the place," Gorman said. "I told you we were right to scout ahead, to get here before Gunn and the woman."

The three hardcases stared down the long vastness from their mountain peak to the tiny figures of Bixby and Charcoal Calf, plunging down the slope far below. Faint puffs of dust rose around the pygmy forms, but it was too far away for them to hear the clatter of their descent.

"What do we do?" Maxwell Lee asked. "Wait till he digs it out, then take him and the Brule?"

"You two split up," Gorman ordered. "Max, you

go around that way, west. Fred, you take the other way, east. And stay on high ground. Watch for Gunn. If he starts closing in, bushwhack him."

Fred Wykoff's narrow eyes gloated, and one hand stole to the stock of the Winchester protruding from its saddle boot. "You don't worry none about Gunn, If I see the son of a bitch, he's wolf meat."

"I'm going down after Bixby," Gorman said. "I'll let him get so close to the gold that I'm real, real sure it's there. Then I'll take him and the Brule, and the gold is all ours."

"Can you handle both of them alone?" Lee asked dully.

"A man's back ain't no competition," Gorman grinned wolfishly, "not for a .44 Colt."

Fallen boulders across a sloping field slowed Pat Bixby's descent. He and the brave rode carefully, picking their way, so as not to risk breaking a horse's leg. The sun broke through scudding rain clouds, the air steamy hot. Bixby's sweat rose up in vapors around his face, a sweet stench.

It took the better part of half an hour for them to make their descent. As they neared the floor of the valley, they could hear the sound of the distant river roaring through its rocky bed. The smell of the mist lingered above the boulders.

Pat Bixby squinted his eyes in the sticky heat. Sweat beaded down his face, stung his lids. The fat man, who had needed an audience all his life, now used Charcoal Calf for that purpose.

"I waited all my life for this," he said. "Stinking

jobs, people looking down on me. Even Deanne. And Jack. He's always been smarter, luckier, the one people turned to. But he's probably dead now. Hell, it don't matter. I'm the one got the gold."

"When you tell Gunn of this, he will take the gold," Charcoal Calf taunted.

Bixby turned around sharply. "Like hell he will!" he bellowed. "I found the goddamned gold! It's mine! All mine!"

"He will take your gold and your woman," Charcoal Calf said. "He already has your woman. Soon he will have your gold."

Bixby pulled his pistol and pointed it at Charcoal Calf. "I should have shot you, you redskinned bastard, the first day we had you." He cocked the gun and the cylinder turned.

"What about the girl?" Charcoal Calf asked.

"What?"

"The girl," Charcoal Calf said. "If you kill me, you will have nothing to trade for the girl."

For a long moment, it looked as if Bixby was unable to make up his mind whether it was worth it or not. Finally, with an audible sigh of frustration, he put his pistol away. Then he turned and saw the gorge again, and when he did so, he thought of the gold, and he laughed.

"You savage son of a bitch," he said. "You're just tryin' to make me mad, make me do somethin' stupid. Well I ain't stupid, see? So you can just keep your mouth shut."

Bixby thought about what the Brule had said. Maybe there was some truth to it. Maybe Gunn would kill him and take the gold. But not if Bixby played it smart.

He thought about what he would do. He would make camp, dig in the spot Jack marked until he found the gold. Then he'd kill the Indian and throw the body in the river. He could always claim it was an accident, but who the hell would care about what happened to an Indian? After that, he'd double back to meet Gunn and Deanne. They'd go find June. After they found the girl, he'd take care of Gunn.

Deanne might not like it, might even put up a protest. But she'd come around. And with the big man out of the way the three Bixbys could come back and pack the gold out. They'd go someplace elegant, someplace like St. Louis or San Francisco. Yeah, San Francisco. They could live like kings there.

A distant echoing roar reached his ears, rolling back and forth from far off, high on the rim above.

Thunder?

Bixby looked at the sky. The sounds repeated themselves, echoing, vicious.

The fat man cocked his head, then recognized the noise.

It was the sound of distant gunfire.

Chapter Seven

Deanne was down somewhere in the high grass. Gunn couldn't see her.

The first shot hit her horse in the side. The dun screamed, reared up, then pitched sideways hurling the woman free.

A violent battering of shots filled the air with lead. Gunn stayed busy keeping to his own cover. He didn't know whether the woman was badly hurt or not.

The big Walker spooked off down the slope, followed by the pack mule.

Gunn rolled wildly through the grass, which partly exposed him, tried to get to the rim of an ancient buffalo wallow.

Slugs dug into the earth all around him as he threw his body over the rutted lip of the depression and tumbled down inside, getting clear of the line of immediate fire.

A thudding bullet threw rock chips in his face. He cursed and spit dirt and blood, then crawled back up the side of the wallow to risk a brief peek in the direction of the gunshots.

The two of them had been halfway up the long

hillside, climbing hard. The canyon rim loomed ahead six hundred yards or more.

Somewhere up there in the scattered boulders, the rifleman waited.

Gunn peered up there now, but couldn't spot the sniper. The unseen man had Gunn pinned down.

There was the sound of an angry hornet, then a rifle slug dug into the dirt just inches away. He ducked, and tasted blood where he had bitten his tongue. He didn't know who it was, but he was pretty damned good with a rifle.

Gunn unsheathed his Winchester when he dismounted, heard its sharp saw as it whispered from the sheath. He levered a shell into the chamber, then scanned his surroundings with narrowed eyes.

The wallow was about a hundred yards in diameter, slightly sloping with the hillside. Gunn lay on the uphill, higher end. The wallow was old, hadn't been used for a long time, its dusty, central pit studded with a few saplings. Along much of its rim, high grass and a few firs stood two or three feet tall.

The rifleman's position, above Gunn's position, gave him full view of his target. Gunn knew that the moment he tried to climb over the lip anywhere around the wallow, he would be exposed to deadly rifle fire.

Except for one place.

About thirty feet to Gunn's right, erosion had partly uncovered a sandstone boulder the size of a small shed. The rock leaned out away from the wallow, tipped precariously, as if the slightest pressure might start it rolling down the far side into the high grass below.

A clump of little fir trees guarded the near side of the boulder, a poplar about six feet tall, the far side.

Gunn studied the situation. The odds were long, but they were better than no odds at all.

He called out, his voice a low rasp in his throat. "Deanne?"

A small voice called back, faint and fearful. "I'm here."

"Are you hurt?"

"I don't think so. I got banged up a little in the fall, but I don't think I broke anything?"

Gunn breathed a sigh of relief. "You weren't hit?"

"No."

"Deanne, listen to me. He must not see you in those weeds or he'd be firing. Stay still. Don't move. Whatever happens, don't move!"

"I understand." Her voice told him she was frightened, but under control. That was good. He didn't have time now to worry too much about her.

Gunn stayed below the lip of the wallow, then edged his way carefully around to the right. Far enough from the top, he hunkered down, moved along on bent legs. He reached a spot below the boulder, then examined the base of the large rock.

It was bigger than he thought, the size of a small barn. Wind and rain had carved most of the loamy dirt away from its bottom, leaving it perched on a lip of soft earth.

Gunn considered his plan, but couldn't come up with a better one. Not with the rifleman up there, still waiting.

Gunn sat in the dirt and placed the Winchester down close beside his thigh, then braced his booted feet in the soft dirt below the boulder.

He put his shoulder up under the rounded, sandy slope of the great rock, applied pressure, lifted, strained.

The boulder didn't budge, not an inch.

Sweat oozed through Gunn's pores. He reset his feet a little higher, coiled thick leg and back muscles against the weight. He set his shoulder again, his hands against the warm, gritty rock, and heaved.

Nothing happened.

Gunn applied more muscle. His legs ached under the strain. The left shoulder of his shirt popped at its seam, and sweat gushed down his face and sides. His back felt like it was breaking, his lungs were nearly bursting with the exertion. He had known a man once who tried to pick up a wagon. He had been a big man, young and powerful beyond belief. But the wagon had weighed a ton or more. The young giant heaved, and heaved again, until blood had burst from his nostrils and ears. He had let out a terrible cry, then dropped dead on the spot.

Gunn felt like his heart would burst open.

"Move, damn you!" he muttered and gave a final, convulsive shove.

The huge boulder groaned in the earth, began to tip.

He grabbed the Winchester with his free hand, still applied pressure to the rock with his right.

The boulder lost its balance. It started to move slowly, rolling over the far side of the rim.

Dirt puffed up. A tuft of prairie grass the size of a man's hand tore loose and flipped into the air. The boulder moved another few inches and then was overbalanced. Great clods of dirt flew up. Then the rock began to tip over and roll.

As the great rock moved, Gunn moved with it, putting it between himself and the distant gunman.

The boulder thundered over the edge and started down, picking up speed. Gunn ran along with the rock keeping well behind it, and well out of sight, and under cover from the hidden rifleman. The stone moved faster, making a rumbling sound now, like a small herd of buffalo. By now Gunn was having to run as fast as he could just to keep up with it. Finally the boulder picked up speed and he couldn't keep up anymore, but by then he was concealed in the flying dirt and dust.

The boulder crunched into the high grass and clumps of baby evergreens on the far side of the wallow.

Gunn dove clear and threw himself headfirst into a little erosion gully as the boulder thundered on down, bounced high into the air, came down to flatten some firs, then careened to a halt in the middle of a grassy slope.

Gunn gasped for wind, sucking in great, heaving breaths. He lay very still, with his cheek pressed into the cool earth on the shady side of the trench.

There were no gunshots from above.

The shooter had likely seen the rock move, perhaps wondered what it was for, but he hadn't seen Gunn. Not yet.

Gunn forced himself to be still, patient. Finally his heart stopped its violent hammering and his wind returned. Sweat soaked his shirt, caked the powdery yellow dust. He itched all over and the taste in his mouth was foul. But he had gotten out of the wallow, and now he knew where the shooter was. And maybe, the shooter did not know Gunn was no longer in the buffalo wallow.

With infinite patience and stealth, Gunn raised his head an inch at a time until he could peer out through the weeds cloaking the little gully. He looked upslope toward the rifleman's hiding place without moving his body.

Slowly he brought the Winchester up from his side, got it positioned in the brush ahead of him, and sighted along its dusty, blued barrel toward the rim above.

Minutes passed.

Flies buzzed, landed on hair legs, walked around, biting through Gunn's sweat. His bad knee ached from the run and both of his elbows were bleeding.

His searching eyes watched for any slight movement, in his mind he pleaded with the unseen bushwhacker to show himself. The advantage was with him now, and he took comfort in that. Deanne was uninjured and safe. He could wait all day if he had to, because he was a man who had learned patience.

His eyes stung from the sweat and the unblinking study of the rim, but he didn't dare move to rub them.

He waited longer, then caught a shadow of movement. His body filled with tension, almost an excitement, an end to the long moments of waiting.

Up on the rim, slightly to his left, from behind a clump of rocks, a glimmer, a dark form moved. Then moved again.

Gunn breathed shallow, light gasps. He gently

heeled back the hammer on the rifle, depressed the trigger slightly to muffle the sound of the sear engaging. He waited, ready.

Again the shadow moved. It became the outline of a man's hat, then the arms and chest to go with it.

The shaded form moved cautiously, slowly. Whoever it was was no amateur in setting up an ambush. He made no abrupt movements, kept himself off the crest, kept himself under cover as much as possible. But if Gunn had sized him up, his adversary had been less cautious, more confident that he was the better of the two men in the contest. He couldn't know that Gunn was watching with the cunning intensity of a rattlesnake, and had detected the small, smooth movement.

The man moved forward, partly exposing himself. He needed to look down on what had happened. He used himself as bait to draw out fire from below.

But Gunn still waited.

The shadow moved out a little farther, peered down. Gunn couldn't see his face, but he could see the outline of his head under the broad brim of the hat.

It wouldn't be an impossible shot now. It would be very difficult, but not impossible.

Gunn raised the barrel of the Winchester a few inches and drew a bead.

But the bushwhacker was even better than Gunn thought. He had caught the slight movement and darted back behind the rocks just as Gunn fired.

The bullet hit the rock just beside the rifleman's head, then, smashed and tumbling, whined off into space as the gunman slipped out of sight.

Gunn had to move now. His position had been given away by the shot. He scrambled to his feet, threw himself forward and ran toward the assailant. A clump of brush a few paces ahead offered concealment.

The trajectory of a Winchester .44 is such that if it is aimed at a target 200 yards away, at 100 yards, the bullet is six feet above the line of sight. At 175 yards, the trajectory would still be high enough to give him some leeway.

From behind the rocks above came puffs of smoke. Gunn could hear the bullets whistling overhead, and he knew that the gunman was shooting at where Gunn had been.

Gunn had enough room now to raise himself slightly and fire off four rounds as fast as he could work the rifle. A hoarse cry burst from the rocks above after the third shot. Gunn threw himself down flat.

Silence fell.

Gunn counted to a hundred, then started over.

After agonizing minutes, another sound came. Rifle and revolver fire, booming, hollow, somewhere a mile or two away.

It came from over the rim, in the valley beyond.

The outburst was followed by a deep silence.

Another minute crept by.

Gunn heard distant hoofbeats on the far side of the rim above. Fading away.

The bushwhacker was hightailing it.

From somewhere, far off, came a single rifle shot.

Then more silence.

Caution told Gunn to wait, as before. It could be a

trick. But there was no time to wait now. He would just have to take his chances.

He took a deep breath, raised himself out of the brush, and presented a target.

Nothing happened.

Gunn stood up. Still nothing.

He turned and ran back to the far side of the wallow, where Deanne's horse lay dead.

"Deanne?" he called sharply.

She raised herself from the deep grass. Her face was the color of old paper with a smudge of blood on her cheek and chin.

Gunn helped her to her feet. "Are you all right?"

She grasped her left arm. "I sprained it or something. I don't think it's broken."

"Can you fetch Esquire and the mule?" he asked.

Deanne nodded and looked downhill where the two animals were grazing as contentedly as though nothing had happened. Nothing at all.

Gunn pointed to the west, downslope. "Bring them around that way. Go slow. Unless I'm on top, signalling you to come on, you're to climb that knoll and get back to the caves as fast as you can. And hide there."

"What about you?" she demanded.

"I've got some work to do." Gunn turned away from her and started jogging back up the hill.

Chapter Eight

Pat Bixby heard the distant sound of gunshots.

He knew they meant trouble. Serious trouble.

They came from behind him somewhere, beyond the rim. It could mean Gunn and Deanne were being attacked by Indians, though he doubted that. There wasn't enough gunfire for an Indian attack. But if not Indians, then who?

The fat man was puzzled. He pulled out his old Navy revolver and leveled it unsteadily on Charcoal Calf.

"Turn around," he ordered. "We're heading back. And take it slow and easy, until I figure out what's going on."

Inside, Bixby was boiling with a nameless fear.

Lucas Gorman heard, too. He cursed under his breath, thought the gunshots in the distance couldn't have come at a worse time.

He and Maxwell Lee had found a place of concealment within three hundred yards of the track Bixby was following. Through his glass from the lookout in the rocks, Gorman had seen Bixby's quickening pace, had measured his high state of excitement. He knew that Bixby was leading them straight to the treasure of gold. And with Fred Wykoff lying in wait to ambush Gunn if he came up, Gorman was confident their scheme would bear fruit.

But the gunshots changed everything.

Gorman ducked low, pushed Lee down with him. Bixby and the Indian swung their horses around.

"Son of a bitch!" Gorman swore under his breath. "Now he's goin' to be nervous and on the lookout for somethin'."

Gorman waited. If there were no more shots fired, he could be sure that Wykoff had finished off the troublesome Gunn. Bixby might be alert, but the odds would be three against him and the unarmed brave. Fish in a barrel, that's what it would be.

Then more shots echoed. A volley. Two different weapons.

Bixby and the Brule turned, started back the way they'd come. Back toward Gorman and Lee.

"Shit!" Gorman swore as he grabbed Lee's arm. "C'mon, let's get back to the horses. I need to know what the hell's goin' on."

The two men left the way they'd come, riding through a narrow arroyo that dissected the hillside. The gully kept them out of view from Bixby and the Brule. Gorman punished his horse, driving his spurs in deeply to force him to climb.

More shots rang out from above.

Gorman and Lee topped the valley wall into a grove of pines. Wykoff met them, riding hard.

The fleeing rider reined in wildly, pulling the roan down on its haunches in the loose dirt and pine needles. Wykoff was covered with rock dust, his nostrils were distended, the whites of his eyes shining crazily.

"What happened?" Gorman demanded.

"I missed him. He pulled some trick with a boulder and got outta the wallow where I had him pinned down. I might of got the woman, dunno for sure."

"To hell with the woman!" Gorman shouted. "Where's Gunn?"

"I'm not sure. He may be chasing after me."

Gorman spat, then looked around. Ahead was the rim with Gunn somewhere beyond. Below, unseen, rode Bixby and the Indian boy.

"Shit," Gorman said, trying to get his rage under control, "We just about had it. He'd nearly found the gold when you started shooting."

"What the hell was I supposed to do?" Wykoff asked, stung by Gorman's remark. "You said keep an eye open for Gunn and take 'im out if I saw him comin'. Well, I saw him comin'. He was trailin' Bixby and that Injun like he was followin' a railroad track. Another five minutes 'n he'd'a been on top of 'em. What would you have done then?"

"All right, all right," Gorman said. He sighed. "We better get outta here for now. Come on, we can go up that way." He pointed to a narrow trail leading away from the rim.

"We're givin' up?" Maxwell Lee asked, not believing Gorman.

"No, goddamnit, we're not givin' up," Gorman snapped. "We're just pulling back to save our ass and figure out a better way to attack next time. Now c'mon. Move!"

Gunn reached the rim of the valley and looked down. Pat Bixby, the Brule and the pack mule rode the trail, coming up toward him.

Gunn waited, his glance raking every inch of the panoramic view.

Bixby rode hard, punishing the mare under him. His eyes were wide, and his skin flushed red with excitement.

"What happened? I heard shooting. You all right? Where's Deanne?"

"She's all right," Gunn clipped. "We got bushwhacked by somebody."

"You did? Where is he?" Bixby wheeled around, looking. "I hope you killed the son of a bitch!"

"He got away," Gunn stated.

"Injun or white?"

"White."

"Why would a white man be out here, attacking people like us?"

"I've got a pretty good idea why," Gunn answered.

"Why?"

"Well, now, you just think about it, Bixby," Gunn said. "You spent the winter in town, you spent a lot of time in the saloon, didn't you?"

"Well, what if I did? We were stuck there, couldn't

go anywhere 'till the weather broke. But I didn't make no enemies there . . . I didn't give anybody any call to come after me. If you ask me, the feller was after you. You're a strange man, a quiet man, like as not you've made plenty of enemies in your life time."

"I'm sure I have," Gunn agreed. "But he wasn't after me."

"What, then?"

"Bixby, while you were spending the winter, waiting for the weather to break, entertaining all your saloon friends, did you ever mention the gold? Or your brother? Did you ever tell anyone you had a map to a gold mine?"

"I never mentioned the map!" Bixby said resolutely.

"I see. But you did talk about the gold? Maybe you said something like, there's so much gold in the Black Hills that you could find gold nuggets the size of robin's eggs, clinging to the roots of grass. Lieutenant Slater told me the story. Where would he have heard it, if not from you?"

Bixby squirmed, and pulled at the collar, which had suddenly grown too tight around his neck.

"I don't know," Bixby said. He fished out his bottle, pulled the cork, took a couple of swallows, then re-corked it and put the bottle back in his rear pocket. "Maybe I said somethin' like that, once or twice."

"Now, do you want to take a guess as to why we were followed?"

"Followed? You think the fella that bushwhacked you, followed us?"

"Not just him. I've found sign for three white men.

I suspect they followed us all the way from Laramie. When you were shooting off your mouth back in the saloons, last winter, these damn fools heard you. And what's worse, they believed you."

"Where do you reckon they are now?" Bixby asked contritely.

"The one who tried to bushwhack me got away. I imagine he joined the others, and they've pulled back to figure what to do next. They aren't a surprise to us anymore, so, whatever idea they had in mind for us, it will have to be changed."

Bixby's face flushed even redder. "We can't just leave 'em be, Gunn! We got to track 'em down! We got to get rid of 'em!"

"Don't be such a fool, Bixby," Gunn said. "You split our party to go off chasing that pot of gold. That gave these three hoots a chance to slip ahead of me, trail you. If I hadn't come along when I did, they would've bushwhacked you instead." Gunn paused, fixed Bixby with his slate-colored eyes. "If they had, you'd be dead right now. You and the Indian boy. They damn sure wouldn't spare him."

"Well, I'm not dead," Bixby flared. "I'm alive! Alive and kicking!"

"Did you find the gold?"

"No," Bixby answered quickly. "I haven't found the spot on the map yet." Bixby's eyes narrowed, and a thin veneer of perspiration broke out on his lip. He looked down, avoiding Gunn's gaze.

Gunn looked at Charcoal Calf.

"What about it, Charcoal Calf? Did the white man find the gold?"

"He has found the place where he believes the gold to be," Charcoal Calf answered. "But he had not found the gold. I think he does not want to find the gold."

"Why would you say that? That's all in the hell he's had on his mind since we started on this journey."

"He does not want to find the gold because I told him, when he finds the gold, you will kill him and take the gold and his woman."

"You talk a lot, don't say much," Gunn said.

"He did not believe me," Charcoal Calf went on.

"You know what he's doin' don't you?" Bixby asked quickly. "He's trying to separate us, get us to goin' one at the other. It's a trick, you see. He gets us to fightin', then he can get away."

"You may be right, Bixby," Gunn said. But the seeds had been planted. The woman was between them and so was the gold.

The gold was close, very close.

But Stone Legs and his Brules were getting farther away every minute.

"Well," Gunn said, confronting Bixby, "it's about time to fish, or cut bait. Now which will it be?" he asked.

"Which will it be? What do you mean, which will it be?" Bixby asked, confused by Gunn's statement.

"Either we look for your brother and the gold, or we make tracks after Stone Legs."

"Why," Bixby blustered, "we go after my daughter, of course."

"No more going off alone," Gunn ordered.

"All right, no more going off alone. If there are

three men out there after me, I don't want to be alone, anyway."

Deanne arrived then, riding the mule and leading Esquire up the narrow rock trail from the flats below. Her face was ashen. Her eyes dark, and angry.

"Deanne!" Bixby breathed, then dismounted and started toward her with his thick arms outstretched. "It's good to see you're safe." He noticed then, that she was riding the mule. "Where's your horse?"

"Dead," Deanne said flatly. "Where were you?"

"What? Why I . . ."

"Where were you, Pat? Why didn't you come back and try to find us last night? We were almost killed because we were looking for you, trying to find out if you were all right?"

"I was never better," Bixby reasoned. "We were trailing Stone Legs last night. We followed him too far, when we turned back it was already dark, too late to find you. We camped out on our own."

"You weren't looking for June," Deanne seethed. "You were looking for gold. Nothing else matters to you any more."

"Deanne! That isn't true."

Gunn stepped in. "All right, this isn't getting us anywhere," he said. "The trail is getting cold. We'd better get on it, or we're going to lose him entirely."

"What about the men trailing us?" Bixby asked.

"We'll keep an eye open, but I think they'll stay out of sight and wait for the right chance to ambush us. If we're smart, we won't give them that chance." Gunn paused. "Now let's get moving."

"Whatever you say, Gunn," Bixby replied, relieved

that he wasn't questioned any further about the gold.

The small caravan retraced part of their trail then cut back below the twin peaks, where Gunn picked up Stone Legs's trail again. The overcast sky which had been with them for two days now, finally began to spill some of its water. It wasn't a hard, driving rain, but a steady drizzle which plastered their hair down, soaked through their clothes, and made tracking more difficult.

There were times when Gunn would lose the trail, and have to hunt to find it again. Once he rode two miles up and down a stream to find where the Brules, after wading their ponies to throw him off, had come back out on the same side of the stream and headed north again.

The trail meandered, uncertain, as if Stone Legs had no destination. Gunn knew better. The deeper the crafty Indian took them into the Black Hills, the greater the chance of encountering another, larger band of Sioux. A band capable of mounting an attack that Gunn and his little group could not withstand.

But Gunn had no choice. He was committed to find June, so they pressed on.

The rain continued throughout the day, finally stopping just before nightfall. The sun dipped out of the clouds and passed through a clear band of sky before setting in one final burst of red and gold.

Gunn called camp, and the four wet riders dried out as best they could. Charcoal Calf, who was wearing the least amount of clothing, had the easiest time of it, and he chuckled once or twice as he saw Gunn and Bixby take off their shirts to wring the water out of them. Deanne, of course, couldn't even do that.

Supper was jerky and coffee, the coffee taken more for warmth than anything else, because after nightfall, the wet clothes made them shiver with chill. Deanne, exhausted and in pain from her wrenched arm, finally sank into a restless sleep, swaddled in a soggy blanket, her face pale in the winking light of the campfire.

Charcoal Calf, unmoving where he was tied against a tree, slumped lower in his bonds, his breathing low and steady.

Bixby rolled his portly frame into a curled position, close to the scant warmth of the fire embers and began to snore gently.

Gunn half-dozed sitting up. Sleep tugged at his eyelids, the day's events piled up on him. He ached to lie down, forced himself erect to avoid deep sleep, his Winchester across his knees.

The tall man grew cold in the night. He was not sure if he was asleep or awake, but he knew he was alert. He noted the night prowling of a coyote and her pups, saw the airborne attack of a burrowing owl against a tiny grasshopper mouse, and sensed the nocturnal exploration of a spadefoot toad.

The endless night dragged on, a clock tick at a time. Gunn fought the intense weariness and fatigue. He could doze in the saddle tomorrow.

The depths of night and the earliest gray of dawn

were the times of danger.

He dozed lightly, nodding off, awakening again, to look into the night. He built a smoke and walked stiffly out of the camp circle to smoke. Then returned, slumped down again.

It was so damned quiet, he began to worry.

Something was not right, but he couldn't put a name to it.

He just knew that something was wrong.

Chapter Nine

The shrieking cry of a killdeer pierced the early morning calm. Nearby, its mate answered the call. The brown and white birds fluttered up out of a high stand of gamma grass about fifty yards away, then winged off in startled flight. Nearby, a prairie dog sounded a warning bark, its bark repeated by dozens of other prairie dogs which were within earshot of the warning. The barks turned to high-pitched whistles of terror.

Gunn's eyes opened abruptly. It wasn't the din of the prairie dogs which had alerted him. He knew that sometimes an entire prairie dog colony would work itself into a frenzy because one of them barked at a butterfly. What had alerted Gunn was nothing more frightening than a feeding call.

He heard the clear sweet warble of a longspur. It was a normal sound on the Wyoming plains, except immediately after a rain. The birds so disliked moisture that after rains they abandon their own territory and seek dry ground, returning only when the grass is dry. Yet, here was a longspur, clearly calling from somewhere in the wet, high grass nearby.

Maybe. There was something not quite right about it, and the feeling of the night before, the feeling that something was wrong, persisted. Over the years, the tall man had trained himself to pay close attention to every sound, every movement, every hunch.

Gunn did not move his body, but glanced over at the sleeping Brule. The Indian boy sat slumped in his bonds, his head down on his chest. Gunn watched the youth. The boy's eyes were closed, but his lips were pursed for a whistle.

The longspur was answered, not by another longspur, but by Charcoal Calf. So much for the mystery of why a longspur would stay in wet grass. Charcoal Calf was answering a signal from one of Stone Legs's warriors. The Sioux had come, perhaps had been there most of the night, to steal the horses, perhaps, to take scalps, maybe.

Gunn eased his body into a slow roll around to the side of the tree that had been his leaning post. He landed on his hands and knees, rose silently, and slipped into the brush.

He moved quickly and quietly through the shadows of the fir trees, toward the direction of the calling Brule.

Gunn stepped carefully over rocks as he worked his way toward the horses, walking in stocking feet over the soft needles. He could see his horse's head through the firs, and noticed by the way Esquire's ears were twitching that he was as confused by the sound as Gunn had been. Esquire had one advantage over Gunn. Esquire's hearing was more acute, and though he couldn't figure out what was making the sound, he knew where it was, and he was looking right toward it.

Gunn moved cautiously, watching the horse for direction. He paused after each step, not wanting to press the Indian and thus alert him. By now, Gunn had a pretty good idea where the Brule was concealed. He was sure that the brave was alone. The animals would have raised more of a ruckus if there were several Indians around.

Gunn dropped his hand to the soft leather scabbard at his side, wrapped his hand around the smooth bone handle of the Mexican knife, the one that bore the legend in Spanish: *No me saques sin razon, ni mi guardes sin honor*.

"Do not draw me without reason, nor keep me without honor."

It had been a gift from a Mexican friend a long time ago . . .

The knife was a Bowie-type, honed on both edges, wide bladed, sharp and deadly, with a blood gutter on either side.

Gunn waited for a long, silent, moment. He could feel the heat of the sun on his back. It was up full disc now, and had already turned from early morning red to shimmering gold. Though it was not yet blinding to the eyes, it had begun warming the earth, bringing the daytime creatures to life. Grasshoppers leaped from stem to blade, dragonflies hovered over shining mud puddles, lizards scurried out onto rocks to lie in the sun. One of the horses stamped a foot and switched a tail, warning a fly away.

Esquire's head came up higher. The Brule was moving.

A clump of weeds rustled quietly, locating the Indian for Gunn. Gunn crouched over, moved gingerly toward the weeds.

The Brule leaped up from the ground twenty feet ahead of him. He let out a blood-curdling scream and rushed toward Gunn, a knife in his right hand, held low, point forward, wicked, and dangerous.

The brave's disfigured left hand caught Gunn's eye. The fingers were knotted and misshapen, the thumb crippled and useless against the back of his hand.

"Broken Hand!" Gunn muttered. He had heard of the Indian, of the hate that drove him. He was always ready to kill a white man. Any white man.

A few years earlier, in a raid on a settlement of homesteaders, the brave had been captured. The God-fearing folks who held him didn't kill him, but smashed his left hand with an axe handle. Then they turned him loose to go back to his people a cripple. They thought the shame of being a cripple would stop his warring. They didn't consider the strength a man can draw from hate. Broken Hand emerged from that encounter as one of the most feared of all Red Cloud's warriors. He was Stone Legs's sub-chief, a man who knew no fear, who killed without hesitation.

The Brule was upon Gunn almost before he realized it, slashing a long, brutal arc with his knife. Broken Hand was an experienced knife fighter, and he knew that the advantage was often with the man who struck first, attacking quickly, while his opponent was still off guard. In nine fights out of ten, the fight would already be over now, but Gunn was that one in ten whose courage, reflex and skill were merged. He moved his belly back at the last instant. Despite Gunn's quick reaction, he still felt the point of the Indian's knife cutting through his shirt, pricking his skin with a wound no deeper than that which would be inflicted by a thorny branch. Had his reaction been a split second later, the Indian would have opened his belly and spilled his insides onto the ground.

Gunn knew a few tricks as well, and even as Broken Hand was slashing at him, Gunn was able to slip his own knife in and open a long gash on Broken Hand's side. The Indian's wound was deeper than Gunn's, and a bright spill of red blood began to roll down over his breechcloth and buckskin trousers.

Back in the camp, Gunn's companions had been awakened by the Sioux's battle cry. Deanne screamed and Bixby called out in surprise. They jumped to their feet to watch as Gunn and Broken Hand met in mortal combat.

The opening thrusts of the battle had told the combatants a great deal about each other. Both had entered the fray confident of each one's own superiority. Now each of them knew that they were facing an adversary whose skill with a knife was equal to his own. They could afford no mistakes, would give no quarter.

Broken Hand and Gunn both stalked each other on the balls of their feet, dancing around in a little circle, crouched, torsos bent at the waist, right arms out, blades projecting from across the upturned palm between the thumb and index finger. They eyed one another warily, neither willing to commit himself yet, for fear either would leave themselves open for a counter thrust.

"*Hoo ee kh'pay ya wee chah yah po!*" Broken Hand shouted. "*Hu kah, hu kah, hay!*"

"*Hu kah hay!*" Charcoal Calf shouted back.

"You better keep your mouth shut, Injun!" Bixby shouted to Charcoal Calf. " 'Lessen' you want a bullet in your head!"

Gunn shifted his knife to his left hand and feinted with it. The move surprised Broken Hand, and he counter-thrust quickly, giving Gunn the opening he was looking for. Gunn flipped the knife back to his right hand then stepped in and hoved the wide blade into Broken Hand's side, just between the ribs.

They stood together for a few moments, Gunn twisting the blade in the wound, trying to make certain his stab was fatal and shifting his feet to maintain his balance against Broken Hand's final, desperate struggles.

Broken Hand's eyes glazed. He staggered a half step as if trying to pull away from the blade that twisted upward, severed vital bloodlines, cut a path to his heart. Finally, he began to collapse, expelling a long, life-surrendering sigh as he did.

As Gunn felt him going, he turned the knife, blade edge up, letting Broken Hand's body tear itself off by its own weight. He cut deeply along Broken Hand's ribs, disemboweling him. When Broken Hand hit the ground, he flopped once or twice like a wounded animal, then lay still while the contents of his opened stomach spilled into the dirt.

For several seconds, everyone remained quiet and still. Gunn stepped away from Broken Hand's body, still holding the blood-stained blade in his hand. He looked down at the dead Indian, breathing heavily. The fight hadn't been physically exhausting, it was over too fast for that. But it had totally drained him emotionally. He looked into Broken Hand's face. The eyes of the fallen Indian were open and unseeing, and still registered surprise. Broken Hand had not had time to know fear or to feel much pain.

Gunn reached down, cleaned the blade of his knife on Broken Hand's bare leg, then put it back in his sheath.

"Gunn!" Deanne said, seeing the front of his shirt red with blood. "You're hurt?"

"Not much," Gunn answered.

He took the torn shirt off and looked down at the slash across the muscles of his belly. The ridges of muscle had been as effective as his quick reaction, in preventing the cut from being any worse.

Deanne used the shirt to dab at the wound, blotting up the blood and looking at the cut. She touched his skin once, then jerked her fingers back quickly, as if remembering the forbidden passion they had already shared. She took in a quick, little breath, then let it out in a long, audible sigh.

"You were lucky," she finally said.

"Yeah," Gunn answered. He walked over to his saddle bag and took out another shirt, then began slipping it on over the broad chest and muscled stomach. Deanne watched him with eyes which were deep and longing, as if lighted by little red lights, way in the bottom.

Gunn looked over at Charcoal Calf, whose eyes had not left the face of the dead Indian. "He a friend of yours?" Gunn asked.

"He was my brother," Charcoal Calf said. "He was coming for me."

"I'm sorry. I didn't have much choice. You called him in, you know."

"He would've killed you," Charcoal Calf said. "I will kill you if I have the chance."

"Yeah. I reckon so," Gunn said.

Bixby had been so intrigued by the dead Indian, that he had not even noticed the expression in Deanne's eyes as she watched Gunn. Finally Bixby looked over at Charcoal Calf.

"What was that the two of you yelled at each other?" Bixby asked. "That huka hay business? What was that?"

"Nothing," Charcoal Calf said. "It was a battle chant, that's all."

Bixby levered a bullet into the chamber of his rifle and pointed it at Charcoal Calf. "Yeah? Well, I want to know what it was."

"It means you use animals as women," Charcoal Calf said. "It's a thing we say to our enemies."

"Animals as women?"

"Think about it, Bixby," Gunn said drily.

Bixby did think for a moment, then when he realized what it meant, he aimed his rifle at the boy.

"Why, you dirty-talkin' redskinned son of a bitch!" he said. "My wife's here! You can't talk like that in front of my wife!"

Gunn reached Bixby in one long stride. He grabbed the rifle and snatched it out of Bixby's hands.

"Just back off," he said softly.

Bixby pointed at the Indian. "Well, you heard what he said. If you had any decency in you, you wouldn't want that kind of talk goin' on in front of my wife. Using animals as women? That's indecent."

"Nobody knew what the hell they were saying until you brought it up. Let it alone, it's just an Indian war chant, that's all. It doesn't mean anything unless you're stupid enough to let it mean something."

Bixby walked away from the Brule with his lower lip rolled out in a pout. He stood there for a moment, then looked around.

"I don't know why you're takin' up for him, anyway," Bixby said. "He signaled that Indian in here, nearly got us all killed."

Gunn pointed at the dead Indian. "He was just trying to rescue his brother," Gunn said. "We're trying to rescue your daughter. What's the difference?"

"What's the difference?" Bixby gasped, as if stunned by the question. "Well, if you can't see the difference between my darling, sweet daughter, and this half-naked redskin, then I wonder what you're doing here in the first place."

"Pat, for God's sake, shut up," Deanne finally said.

"What?" Bixby asked, surprised by his wife's words.

"At least Mr. Gunn is looking for June. That's

more than I can say for you. All you've had on your mind from the moment we started was finding that gold. I'll not stand here and listen to you harangue a man who is risking his life for us."

Bixby stared at Deanne for a moment, then gradually the anger left his face to be replaced by an expression of genuine shame. He looked at Gunn and sighed.

"I'm sorry, Gunn," he said. "Deanne's right. You are risking your life for us. I was out of line."

"Your apology's accepted," Gunn said. "Now, let's break camp. The sun's getting high. I want you to take Deanne and the boy and back trail it to the valley."

"What? What do you mean?" Deanne asked. "Why are we back trailing?"

"I want you to go back and wait for me. It's getting too dangerous for you to be out here." His tone was final as he sat down to draw on his boots.

The woman squatted on the ground near him. "Gunn, let me go with you," she pleaded. "I'm prepared to take the risks."

"You don't understand," Gunn said. "If I have to look out for all of you, as well as myself, then the risks are greater than I'm prepared to take . . . not for you . . . for me."

"Oh," Deanne said, understanding his meaning then. "I see what you mean. Of course, I had never realized the danger we were putting you in. It's just . . ."

"I know what it is," Gunn said. "It's harder for you to wait than it is for you to be doing something. But believe me, the best thing you can do for June right now is give me some room to work. I can't be worrying about you now. You go back and wait for me. I'll be back soon. And when I do come back, I'll have June with me."

But to himself he said: And if I don't come back, I'll be dead.

Chapter Ten

Gunn squatted on his heels to study the bed of pine needles where Broken Hand had waited for him. Broken Hand had been a medium sized man, heavy enough to make an impression in the pine needles, and thus leave tracks. By studying Broken Hand's tracks here, he would better be able to identify them as he followed back along his trail. He hoped that would lead him directly to Stone Legs.

Gunn stood up and looked around. He saw the fragile twig of a dying bush hanging by a thread of bark. The broken branch swayed in the gentle breeze. Broken Hand had come this way.

After two days of clouds and rain, the weather had finally broken, and this morning was bright and crisp, with the sun already drying up the small puddles and wet bushes. It promised to be a much more pleasant day than the last few had been. And without Pat and Deanne Bixby to slow him down, he should also move faster, and be more productive in his search.

Gunn followed the path Broken Hand might have taken around the edge of the campsite, circled warily, sought any mark on the ground that would furnish a clue. He saw a wad of dead needles crushed, broken evenly at the same length. The pressure of a man's moccasin could've done that.

Gunn continued to follow the almost-invisible trail, spotting a fragile pine bough that had been freshly broken, its wood still pale. The big man brought the twig to his nose and sniffed. The aroma of freshly released pine scent filled his nostrils. Now Gunn knew from which way Broken Hand had approached the camp.

Having established the trail, Gunn returned to where the horses were hobbled. He began saddling Esquire. Deanne came over to talk to him.

"Did you find anything?" she asked.

"I found the way he came," Gunn answered. "I'll follow his trail back, see where it leads me."

"Gunn, when you find her . . . will you tell her that I . . . that we have come for her? I know she'll be frightened, and alone. Maybe if she knows we are here, it'll give her the strength she needs to come through all this."

Gunn swung into the saddle, then looked down at the woman's anxious face. He smiled.

"Don't worry, Deanne," he said. "She's your daughter, isn't she? That gives her all the strength she needs. She's fine. I know she is."

Bixby walked over then, and stood beside his wife, smiling up at Gunn. "We'll go on back to the valley just like you told us to, Gunn," he said. "So if you need us for anything, you just come on back, and you'll find us."

Gunn nodded, then walked the horse out of the

camp until he picked up the trail he had found a few moments earlier, followed it until he found the tracks of one, unshod horse. Broken Hand had been alone.

He got down and studied the pony tracks. The indication from the prints was that the horse had stood for awhile waiting for his master to return. The Indian had probably ground tied the horse, thinking his task would not take much time. There was a circle of impatient tracks, then the horse ambled away. The animal might be searching for water or maybe seeking the other horses in the band.

Gunn's eyes took in the long sweep of the dark hills. He remounted his horse then started off in the direction of the pony. His Winchester rested in one hand, laid across the saddle.

The country began to change. The hills steepened with more rocky outcroppings. The growth was lush, green, deep green. The trail of the pony was obvious, a broken branch here, a turned stone there. The animal dragged its rope reins, left a furrow along the track. The riderless horse was leading Gunn deeper and deeper into the Paha Sapa, the sacred Black Hills.

Gunn had gone a couple of miles, maybe a little farther, when he found Broken Hand's pony. There, a spring of cold, glistening water cascaded out of a broken boulder then pooled in a rock basin. The painted horse, his rope bridle trailing, stood head down, drinking from the pool. The Indian horse swung his head in the direction of the mounted rider, his round eyes rolled until the whites showed.

"Hello, boy," Gunn muttered. "Glad to see you can take care of yourself. You're going to have to now, until someone else claims you." The small horse turned back to the pool, drinking again.

"Hold still for a minute, boy," Gunn said gently to the paint. He nudged the Walker toward the pool. The barebacked horse paid no attention to their approach. He continued to drink, totally undisturbed by their presence.

Gunn dismounted, slipped the Winchester into its boot then joined the two animals at the water hole. He removed his battered felt hat and lowered his face into the cold mountain pool, splashed his head and neck, wiped the excess away with his hands. Then the man drank deep, checked his canteen, emptied its stale contents and refilled it with the fresh, cold water.

Gunn left the two horses to drink their fill while he studied the ground around the pool. If the Indian pony knew this trail to the water hole, maybe it was from habit. Maybe the others passed this way.

Fresh tracks of mountain animals marked the edge of the water. Deer and wild sheep prints mingled with the smaller paw prints. Mixed among the undersized hoof marks were those of more unshod ponies. Fresh tracks. No more than a day old.

Stone Legs. It had to be his band.

Gunn circled the area, widened his search. The prints were confused, mingled, coming and going. He was one hundred yards away when he saw the first, clear set of tracks. There were six or seven unshod horses. The horses bunched, then separated. Three horses had been ridden north on a dim trail, an old route. One of the three horses was carrying a light load.

Gunn smiled. That had to be June Bixby. She was a slim girl and her pony would show the light weight. One of the other ponies showed a fairly substantial weight, as if it were carrying a large, muscular man. Stone Legs was such a man. Stone Legs's band had split up. Now he had only one brave with him. One brave and June Bixby.

The trail headed north, deeper into the hills that threw shadows across the Holy Road.

"You wanna ride the mule, or the Indian boy's pony," Bixby asked his wife.

"The mule and I got along just fine yesterday," Deanne said. "I'll ride the mule."

"Well, we better get on with it," he said. He walked over to Charcoal Calf and looped the rope around the Indian boy's neck. "Come on, boy, we can't be hangin' 'round here all day." He jerked hard, and the boy grimaced in pain.

"Pat," Deanne said. "There's no need for you to be cruel."

"Don't worry," Bixby answered. "I'm not being cruel. Me'n the boy here have an understandin', don't we boy? Now, come on. Get mounted."

Charcoal Calf swung up onto the bareback of his pony, then waited patiently as Bixby grunted and mounted. Bixby led out first, heading along the same trail they had been following all along.

"Wait, Pat. You're headed in the wrong direction, aren't you?" Deanne called ahead.

Bixby looked back at his wife and flashed her a self-satisfied grin. "We're going to follow Gunn. He might need our help."

"For heaven's sake, Pat. The man told us to go back to the valley and wait," she replied, her voice filled with disgust. "You'll . . . we'll only get in his way."

"That fellow don't know everything, Deanne. We might do him some good."

"What about the other men, Pat? The ones that tried to bushwhack Gunn and me. Don't you think they'll follow us? Especially if they think you've found the gold you're always talking about."

"Maybe they will and maybe they won't," he replied. "But just maybe the Indians will take care of them."

"How about us? Wouldn't the Indians take care of us just as well?"

"You worry too much," Bixby said.

"Pat!" the woman shouted. But the man didn't answer this time. Instead, he rode on in the direction he had seen Gunn take.

After a couple of miles, the three riders discovered the water hole where Gunn had found the sign.

Bixby dismounted and searched the area for direction.

As soon as he found the tracks of the big shod horse, the fat man pulled out his map and studied it for a few minutes. Frequently he raised his head to gaze at the surrounding hills.

"Lookee here, Deanne! Just look at this!" The heavy-set man jiggled from one foot to the other in his excitement.

"What is it, Pat?"

"The map. Lookee." Bixby bounced over to his

wife's side, his finger resting atop a spot marked with an X on the dogeared map.

"See that spot there. That's where Jack marked the map. That's where the gold lies. Now look up there at those peaks. There's a stream down below them. That's where Gunn is headed and that's where the gold is. He's a-leading us right to it."

"I thought you already had the place sighted. Back there." The woman gestured with her hand.

"I had the right peak, but the wrong side of it. There it is, Deanne. Plain as day. We're rich! We're rich!" The fat man continued his dance as he refolded the map.

"I thought we were following along to help out Gunn if he needed it," Deanne said.

"Gunn? Hell, Deanne, Gunn don't need our help. He don't want it, you heard him this mornin'. He told us to go on back to the valley and wait for him. No, sir, don't you worry none about Gunn. He'll get along just fine without us."

"You never intended to help anyway, did you?" Deanne asked. "It was the gold, all along. That's what you came out here for. That's what you want."

"Well, what's wrong with a man wantin' to make good for his family?" Bixby asked. "You tell me that. What's wrong with it?"

"What about June, Pat? Have you forgotten about our daughter so soon?"

"Forget my darling June? Deanne, how could you ask such a question?"

"How could I ask? You've talked of nothing but the gold ever since we started after the girl. Don't you think of her out there with those murdering Indians.

It tears at my heart to think of what they might do to her." The woman's voice broke in a sob.

"Deanne, my dear. My old heart is aching for the girl, too. And I want her back, all safe 'n sound, same as you. But just think about it. Iffen we had the gold too, why, it would make this all worthwhile. Now, there's nothin' wrong with what I'm plannin' on doin'. We're goin' in that direction anyway . . . we may as well get all the gold we can."

"Pat, even if you find it, how will you get it out of here? Gold is heavy . . . like lead. There's just the two of us. And don't forget, there are those men who tried to bushwhack us. If they see us with the gold, they'll kill us and take it away from us."

"You let me worry about that. As for the packin' it, we got the boy there to help. And if those fellas do decide to attack us, why, there's Gunn. Gunn likes you, I can tell. He ain't gonna let nothin' happen to you. He might not care all that much 'bout me 'n the gold, but he won't let nothin' happen to you. He'll guard the treasure for us, once we got it in our hands. I know about people like Gunn."

"No, you don't," Deanne said quietly. "You don't know anything at all about the man, and you couldn't learn in a hundred years." She took their canteens over to the spring, emptied the stale water and refilled them. Right now, she wished she had something a little stronger than water.

"Hey, Gorman. Look at this." Maxwell Lee lay on his stomach atop a stone outcropping, a field glass to his eye.

"Yeah? What is it?" came the reply.

"Bixby. He's lookin' at that map and pointin'. I think he's on the trail again."

"Lemme see that," Gorman said and snatched the glass from Lee's hands. He sank to his knees on the ledge as Lee directed the glass.

"See that boulder out there past that clump of firs. Just up and to the left is a little clearing. Bixby's at the far edge of it. See him?"

"Huh? Oh, yeah. I got him now." Gorman was silent for a moment, watching the silent discussion between Bixby and his wife.

"Yeah," Gorman said. "Looks like he's on the trail again." The burly man lowered the glass. "All right, boys, we'll just stay with our first plan. Let Bixby do all the work for us, find the gold and dig it out. All we gotta do is follow him, then help ourselves to it." He chuckled at the prospect.

"What about the woman?" Wykoff asked. He licked his fleshy lips with a saliva-soaked tongue. "We gonna kill her, too?"

Gorman leveled the glass again and saw the woman kneeling beside the spring, filling canteens. He turned and grinned at the anxious Wykoff. "We ain't gonna kill her right off. But I'm goin' first this time. You kilt that woman back where we got the horses without even givin' me a chance."

He looked back down at her. "Oh, oh, they're fixin' to move out. Let's get goin'."

Stone Legs stood just inside the cave and looked at the girl. The cave was bathed in a flickering gold light produced by two burning torches. In the center of the floor, June lay, bound, hand and foot.

Stone Legs wondered why the girl was so important. The whites had followed him far longer and far deeper into the Paha Sapa than he would have ever believed. The tall white man was a devil. His rifle had already killed many of Stone Legs's followers, and now, he believed that Broken Hand was dead as well.

If the tall white man was good enough to kill Broken Hand, then he was a good man indeed. If they met, there would be a good fight, and one of them would die.

"Girl," Stone Legs said, speaking to June. "Who is the man? Who is the tall man who follows?"

"I've told you," June said. "I don't know who he is. He wasn't with our wagon train. He just came along when you attacked us."

"Why would he follow if he does not know you?"

"I don't know," June answered. "I'm telling you the truth. I don't know."

Yellow Nose was standing in the door of the cave. He didn't speak English, so he had no idea of what Stone Legs and the girl were talking about. He asked.

"Are we going to use her?"

"No," Stone Legs answered.

"Why not? She is a captive woman, it is our right."

"We will wait. First, I must kill the tall white man who follows us. Then we will use the captive woman."

"And if the tall white man kills us?" Yellow Nose asked.

"Then she is his woman." Stone Legs looked around toward his prisoner, and spoke in English.

"Yellow Nose says we must make you our woman.

He wants to make you our woman tonight."

June cringed.

"I have told him that I must fight the tall white man who comes for you. If the white man defeats me, you are his woman. If I defeat him, you are my woman."

"I am no one's woman," June said.

Stone Legs walked over to June, then dropped to one knee and looked into her face. His lips wore a faint smirk.

"When I kill the white man," he said. "You will be my woman. You will beg me to come to you."

"Beg you?" June said defiantly. "Not even for my life!"

Chapter Eleven

The terrain unfolded in a series of rolling hills, saltbush shrubs and eroded gullies. As Bixby's small band would crest one hill, there would be others ahead of them, then more still, until it seemed like they were doomed to spend an eternity in the great wasteland.

Occasionally, there would be a feature which would stand out above all others, a rocky plateau undercut by erosion, or mounds of compacted clay, sand gravel and volcanic ash, eroded into unique shapes, and sporting puffs of western salsify on the wisps of sod at its crown. With each of these unique shapes, Bixby would consult his map, and grow more visibly excited.

As they continued on their journey, a series of faults extended out into the plain to the east. A ridge about 200 feet high formed along one of the faults, continuing out into the plain to the east. A ridge about 200 feet high formed along one of the faults, continuing east for as far as they could see. To the north a higher, steep-sided escarpment paralleled the southern ridge, and between these two high ridges, a flat-bottomed valley about five miles wide was formed. A valley created by an ancient river which was not little more than a swiftly flowing stream.

When Bixby saw the stream he nearly lost control of himself. He spurred his horse into a gallop, and, as Charcoal Calf had a rope around his neck, leading to Bixby's horse, the Indian youth had to react quickly to keep from having his neck broken.

Bixby covered the remaining one thousand yards to the creek at a full gallop, bouncing up and down in his saddle, slapping his fat legs against the side of the horse to urge his hapless animal on.

He reined up, just short of the water, then jumped off and ran down into the stream, shouting and screaming insanely.

Deanne's mule refused her urging to move any faster, but she finally arrived a few minutes later, just in time to see Bixby walking up and down the stream, looking into the swiftly flowing water, holding a pan by his side.

"Pat, what is it?" she asked. "What's wrong with you? Are you all right?"

"All right? Am I all right, you say? My God, woman, are you blind? I couldn't be better!" the grizzled man shouted. "Don't you realize what this is? This is the stream Jack marked. This is it! This is where he got all his color. This is a river of gold, woman! A river of gold!" Bixby scooped his pan down into the water and then flung it into the air and let the drops cascade back down on him. He looked over at Charcoal Calf, who was still sitting quietly on his horse, his hands tied to the pommel, the rope around his neck slackened, but still in place.

"You! You goddamned redskinned son of a bitch! You thought I wouldn't find it, didn't you? You thought it was the ravings of a fat man, didn't you? Well, by God, I guess I just showed you and Gunn and all those sons of bitches back in Laramie who didn't believe me. By God, I'm rich!"

Pat, you're raving like a madman," Deanne said.

"Yeah? Well, we'll just see how mad I am. Set up camp, woman!" he called. "We've got work to do!"

"Camp, Pat? The sun is still high. We could ride another two, three hours before dark. We'll lose the trail if we stop now." Her voice pleaded with the man.

Bixby climbed the bank and stomped the water out of his boots. "We'll camp here tonight," he repeated. "Tie the boy to a sapling and get a fire going. I got a feeling that I'm gonna be hungry as a bear by nightfall."

"Pat, if this is really it, you know where it is now. We can come back to it. Come on, let's go find June."

"Quit worryin' about June," Bixby said. "Gunn's lookin' for her. He's better at that sort of thing anyway. You know it, and I know it. Now, just shut up and set up the camp like I told you to. I'm not goin' to lose this chance, not for you, not for Gunn, not for June not for anybody. Do you hear me? Not for anybody!"

Bixby walked up the stream a short distance, looking out into the water for a sand or gravelbar. If there was any gold being carried downstream by the water, it would most likely be found at such a bar where the water would swirl and eddy and drop its heavier sediment to the bottom.

Bixby didn't know the geology behind it, but he

knew that there were certain lodes which were exposed to weather and erosion long enough to break down into crumbling chunks, then fragments, then powder. The gold which was trapped in that powder would be carried downhill by rain and mountain streams. In the foothills of a gold-bearing mountain range, where the swift streams lost the mad rush of energy which had brought them tumbling down from the higher elevations, the gold was released, to reside forever on the stream floor . . . or until a prospector found the treasure.

Bixby found a likely spot no more than twenty yards away from where they had stopped. He knelt down, then submerged his pan, scooping up sand and water. After that he swirled the water around just fast enough to allow it to spin up and spill over the edges of the pan, carrying with it the light sand and silt. After a couple of minutes there was nothing left but the drag, as the heavier residue was called. Bixby fanned out the drag on the bottom of the pan, then saw a little sparkling, comet tail of gold specks clinging to the black sand like powdered goldenrod.

Patrick Bixby was a fool by many men's standards. He drank too much, he talked too much, he was self-centered and oafish. But he had spent a lifetime lusting after gold, and he did know the difference between the yellowish, glittering minerals, such as iron pyrites and mica, which had confused so many greenhorns that such substance was called "fool's gold," and the actual thing. Gold was unmistakable to a man who had dreamed of it, hefted it, bit down on it. Fool's gold often winked at the observer if light struck it at just the right angle. Gold stayed the same, regardless of the angle from which it was viewed. Gold was indestructible, never tarnished, and would shine as brightly when found as it did millions of years ago when it was formed by intense heat and volcanic action, shot through the rock in totally liquid form.

"Color!" he shouted, jumping up excitedly. "I got color in the first pan!"

Bixby picked out the little flecks of color and put them in a small, leather sack. He tried a few more pans, then got impatient and moved further upstream, trying sandbars and eddies until he found more color, this time heavier than the first. He squatted in the stream, unmindful of the water which washed over his hips as he scooped sand from the stream floor.

Deanne watched him, listening to him chuckle, while she made coffee. When the coffee was done she poured a cup and took it over to Charcoal Calf who was sitting quietly where she had tied him to the sapling. He took it without thanks.

"You're welcome," Deanne said, sarcastically. She poured herself a cup, then sat on a rock near the campfire and looked into the flames.

"Woman," Charcoal Calf said.

Deanne looked at Charcoal Calf, and, inexplicably, smiled. Her smile puzzled Charcoal Calf.

"Why do you smile?"

"I'm just amazed that you, a mighty warrior, have finally decided to talk to a woman."

"You are more of a man than your man," Charcoal Calf said.

Deanne brushed her hair back. "Well, I don't know

what to say about that," she said. "I suppose that's a compliment, but I'm not sure if I like it."

Deanne's sarcasm went over Charcoal Calf's head, so he made no attempt to respond to it. Instead, he held out his hands toward her.

"Let me go free," he said.

"So you can kill us both?"

"I will not kill you," Charcoal Calf said.

"But you would kill my husband?"

"It will be better for you if your man is dead," Charcoal Calf said. "Then you can have the man called Gunn."

"No," Deanne said.

Charcoal Calf looked puzzled. "Do you not like the man called Gunn better than the fat man who is your man?"

"No!" Deanne said. "And I don't like this conversation."

"You do not want the fat man killed?"

"No! Of course not! And I don't know what gave you such an idea."

Charcoal Calf was silent for a moment longer.

"Let me go and I will not kill him. I will find your daughter and bring her back to you."

"Don't talk to me any more about letting you go," Deanne said. "I'm not going to do it, and that's final!"

Bixby worked until nightfall, then came back and flopped his soaked bulk beside the campfire. He chuckled happily, stared into the flames.

"This is it, woman. I found it, just like I always said I would. I've already got forty, maybe fifty dollars in gold in my poke. This ain't no ten dollar a day strike. A man could set up sluices and shakers and run five hundred a day over the riffles. I knew it was here all the time. I knew Jack wasn't lying about the gold."

Deanne dished up a tin plate of beans for her husband.

"Pat, that's enough for now, isn't it? I mean, you know it's here, you've proved it. Now you can come back here after we find June." She hoped reason would get to the man.

"Listen, Deanne. We all need the rest. Let's just camp here tomorrow. Then we can go on after June. Gunn's up there by now. Probably already got her and is on his way back. Just one day, Deanne. That's all I need."

She let out a long sigh. One day couldn't hurt too much. Maybe Pat was right. Gunn might have June by now.

Bixby finished his plate, then rolled up in a blanket. Within a few minutes, he was snoring loudly. Deanne looked over at Charcoal Calf. His soft, rhythmic breathing indicated that he, too, was asleep. She watched until the fire burned down to embers, then she lay down and stared up at the vault of stars in the midnight sky. She saw a star falling, and breathed a quick prayer because she had once heard that when a star falls, someone will soon die. She wondered if it would be one of them.

"Shit, I thought the gold would already be dug out and just lyin' there waitin' for us," Maxwell Lee grumbled. He threw blades of grass into the small campfire they had allowed themselves.

"Maybe this ain't all there is," Gorman replied. "And anyway, even if it is, why we can't lose. All we gotta do is just set up here for a spell and watch, and let the fat man do the work for us. When we think he's got enough dust in that little bag he's carryin' with him, we'll just go down there, crack his skull, and take it."

"Well, we can't stay up here forever," Wykoff said. "That sodbuster we taken the horses and food from didn't have enough for us to stay out here too long."

"We'll make out all right. There's game. Fact of the matter is, one of us ought to go out of earshot tomorrow and get some meat. I could go for a little elk meat," Gorman said as he scraped the last of his beans from his plate.

"I'll go," Lee said. "I don't like this settin' and waitin' anyways."

When Charcoal Calf opened his eyes during the night, he blinked several times, because there, sitting cross-legged on the ground between him and the faintly glowing embers of the campfire, was Broken Hand! He didn't know if he was asleep or awake, but it didn't matter, he knew there were some who could see visions while awake, and some who saw visions only while asleep. But all visions should be heeded, for visions were gifts form Wakantanka, the Great Spirit and Giver of Truth. He felt honored to be the receiver of a vision.

"Broken Hand, it is really you!" Charcoal Calf said. "You have come from the world of the Spirits to visit me."

Broken Hand began to speak, and he spoke to Charcoal Calf without fear of being seen or heard by the fat man or his woman. He pointed to the north.

"Hear me, my brother," he said. "In the Moon of Making Fat, in the place called Greasy Grass, there will be a great battle between all the nations of the Dakota and the long knives."

"Tell me of this battle," Charcoal Calf said.

"I have seen soldiers falling like grasshoppers, with their heads down and their hats falling off. They were falling into the Indian village. Wakantanka will give these soldiers to the Sioux to be killed. Many nations of the Sioux will be there. There will be Oglala, Brule, Minneconjou, San Arcs, Blackfeet, and even Cheyenne. There will be a great victory for our people."

Charcoal Calf smiled broadly. "I will go to the place of Greasy Grass," he said. "I will fight at the side of our people."

"How can you speak of fighting when you are the prisoner of a woman and a fat man? How can you speak of fighting when the white man who took my life still lives? There are many things you must do, my brother, before you can join our people in the battle of Greasy Grass."

"I will escape," Charcoal Calf promised. "I will escape tonight."

"My brother, will you listen to me? Will you do only what I say?"

"Yes," Charcoal Calf said.

"You must kill the fat man and the woman. Then you must find the tall man and kill him. Only then, will you be able to join our people in the great battle."

"The woman has been kind to me."

"Are you a dog to be petted by a woman? Are you a horse to listen to kind words?" Broken Hand spat "You must kill her. If you do not do everything I say, Wakantanka will be angry, and you will die before you have become a man."

"I will do everything you say."

"There is a sharp stone on the ground beneath you. Dig it out, and cut your bonds. Kill the fat man and the woman . . . kill the fat man and the woman . . . kill the fat man and the woman."

The word began to grow more faint, and the image shimmered before him, as if he were seeing a reflection in water. Broken Hand disappeared entirely, and Charcoal Calf called aloud for him.

Charcoal Calf woke up with a start, then looked around the campsite. He saw the man and woman sleeping, and the campfire had burned low, just as he knew it would.

Broken Hand! Broken Hand had come to see him!

Charcoal Calf rolled to one side, then began feeling around in the dirt with his hands. He found it! The sharp stone Broken Hand had told him about. It was right there!

Charcoal Calf began sawing at the leather thongs which were tied around his wrist, and after several minutes of work, the thongs were cut in two. Charcoal Calf was free.

Quickly, and quietly, Charcoal Calf freed himself of the remaining bonds, then he moved silently over to Bixby's rifle and pistol. He picked them up and aimed the rifle at the fat man's head.

"You must do exactly as I say," Broken Hand had told him. "You must kill the fat man and the woman."

Charcoal Calf sighted down the rifle and tightened his finger on the trigger. The slack in the trigger was taken out. He waited, then, with a sigh, lowered the rifle. He moved quietly to his pony, and walked him out of camp.

A soft, gray light pushed away the night, and Deanne opened her eyes. She looked over at her husband, then at Charcoal Calf.

Charcoal Calf wasn't there.

"Pat!" she yelled. "Pat, where's Charcoal Calf? Where's the boy?"

The round blanket that was her husband grunted and moved.

"Pat!" Deanne called again. She moved quickly to her husband, and began shaking his shoulder.

He muttered and sat up.

"What is it?" he asked. "What are you shouting about?"

"The Indian boy. Charcoal Calf. He's gone."

"Gone? What do you mean, gone?"

"I mean he's gone. He escaped, during the night!"

Bixby heaved himself out of the bedroll, then looked around for his weapons. "Son of a bitch!" he swore. "He took my rifle, and my pistol." Bixby put his hand to his neck. "We're damn lucky he didn't kill us in our sleep."

"He doesn't want us," Deanne said. "Killing us

would be no accomplishment. I think he's going after Gunn."

"You don't say," Bixby said. He ran his hand through his sleep-tossed hair. "Well, I expect Mr. Gunn can look out for himself."

"What are we going to do now?"

"We're gonna sit tight. Gunn'll be back along any time now. Besides it'll give me a chance to work the stream. I don't intend going anywhere until I have all the gold I can carry." He got up then, and started toward the stream to resume his work.

"Well, I certainly don't intend to sit tight!" Deanne called to him. "Do you hear me? I'm going after Gunn. I'm going after our daughter!"

"You do whatever you feel you have to do," Bixby said. "Take the horse if you want. I'll be here when you come back."

For a moment, and she hated herself for it, she wished Charcoal Calf had killed her husband.

Chapter Twelve

The eastern sky began to grow lighter, first a gray, then a pale silver, and finally a soft pink as dawn broke. Gunn was camped in the cool shadow of Crows Nest Peak. The last morning star made a bright pinpoint of light over the Bear Lodge Mountains, lying in a purple line, far to the west.

The coals from his campfire of the night before were still glowing, and he threw chunks of dried cottonwood on it and stirred the fire into crackling flames which danced against the bottom of the suspended coffee pot. A rustle of wind through leaves caused him to look up just in time to see a redtail hawk diving on its prey. The hawk swooped back into the air carrying a tiny chipmunk, kicking fearfully in the hawk's claws. A hognose snake struck at a lizard beneath a nearby stand of prairie asters, which were themselves being choked out by curly buffalo grass and blue gamma.

Gunn poured himself a cup of coffee and sat down to enjoy it. It was black and steaming and he had to blow on it before he could suck it through his lips. He watched the sun peak above the Black Hills, then beam its rays brightly down onto the plains. Today, he would find Stone Legs.

Gunn wasn't depending on any sort of hunch or intuition for his belief. Before it grew too dark to track, last night, there was a growing body of evidence that Stone Legs wanted to be found. The tracks were easier to follow now. Stone Legs no longer covered his trail, no longer made elusive cuts across the rocky slopes of the sacred Black Hills. The cunning warrior seemed to be inviting the lone tracker to a meeting, a council with death.

Gunn stood up and stretched to work out the kinks of spending the night on the ground, then he tossed out the last dregs of his third cup of coffee. He emptied his pot and returned it to the saddlebag, put out his fire. He saddled and cinched up Esquire and rode on. Somewhere ahead, Gunn knew, Stone Legs was waiting for him.

The cave where Stone Legs, Yellow Nose and June had passed the night, was not an ancient cavern caused by some geological fault, but had been formed by centuries of swirling water and wind-whipped sandstone. Now, Stone Legs stood at the mouth of the cave and looked past a barren pinnacle toward the direction from which his pursuer would be coming. Today, Stone Legs would let the tracker find him. Today, they would fight. Today was a good day to die.

Stone Legs thought back over his life, and recalled many of the brave deeds he had done. He remembered once, when his village needed more horses, and decided to get them from the Crows. The Crows were traditional enemies of the Sioux, and a raid on a Crow village was an exciting undertaking, because the Crows were courageous fighters and worthy opponents.

Stone Legs had prepared himself for the battle, painting his body, making medicine, and dancing, then he joined the other warriors as they left on their raid. Raiding for horses was a sport, but it was a dangerous sport. It could bring a warrior reputation and power, or humiliation and shame. It could also bring death, but Stone Legs didn't even consider that as a possibility.

Stone Legs and the others reached the Crow camp on foot, then, with great stealth, managed to take a dozen horses and sneak away from the camp. Soon, however, the Crows discovered their loss, and they sent a war party after Stone Legs and his fellow raiders. The Sioux were slowed by the horses they were trying to herd, so the Crows soon caught up with them. Stone Legs and the others had no choice but to stand and fight.

When the Crows found the little band of raiders, they saw that they had the Sioux greatly outnumbered, so they charged. The leader of the Sioux band advised the others to release the horses and retreat, but Stone Legs jumped off his horse, and ran toward the nearest, charging Crow.

When the Crow saw Stone Legs challenging him, he jumped off his own horse and answered the challenge. The Crow was a chief, Stone Legs merely a novice warrior. Suddenly, the chief stopped running and raised his rifle to aim at Stone Legs. Stone Legs raised his own rifle and they both fired at the same time. The Crow's bullet missed, Stone Legs's bullet found its mark. Stone Legs drew his knife, raced forward, and plunged it into the Crow chief's heart. The rest of the Crows, seeing Stone Legs's medicine, turned and ran. Because of Stone Legs's valor, the Sioux saved the horses they had stolen.

As a result of that fight, Stone Legs was made a member of the Midnight Strong Hearts, an elite warrior society. As a member of the Midnight Strong Hearts, Stone Legs was sworn to never surrender . . . and to fight always with valor and honor.

For the first few years of Stone Legs's membership in the warrior society, he followed its precepts in battle with the Crow. He never fought against the white man. In fact, he saw very few of them. There was an occasional hunter or trapper who passed through, but the hunter or trapper took very little game, and was valuable as a source of trade for the Indians. Stone Legs tolerated their presence.

Then gold was discovered, and the white men began coming in larger and larger numbers. With more white men, there was less room for Indians. The white men took care of that problem by killing Indians. Among those killed were Stone Legs's entire family.

From that moment on, all of Stone Legs's skills had been dedicated to killing white men. Until now, he had never met a white man who taxed his ability, or who posed enough of a threat to challenge the skills of a warrior of the Strong Hearts society. But the man who had been trailing him for the last several days, the man who had already killed so many of his warriors, was an enemy worthy of becoming a member of the Strong Heart society. If only he was Lakota. But maybe that did not matter so much. If he was brave, that was enough. He was sure this one was brave.

Let him come, Stone Legs thought.

As Gunn rode along the relentless trail after Stone Legs, he thought of the tales he had heard of the Old Ones, the Ones Who Walked Before, in the Paha Sapa. White men who had dared travel the forbidden Holy Road told of disappearing moccasin tracks, mutilated horses, men going crazy, aging years in a few weeks. Men had disappeared, never returned from the Black Hills. Bodies had been found, dead for no apparent reason.

The Paha Sapa was a magnificent, mysterious country; a lonely place of whispering winds and rock palisades. Long slopes heavy with dark evergreens gave the Black Hills their name.

Gunn descended a fluted escarpment, and felt a sudden cold gust of chilling air. There was no apparent reason for the sudden drop in temperature, and Gunn felt the hackles on the back of his neck stand up at the strange sensation. Esquire pricked his ears, faltered at the blast of icy wind. The horse seemed to sense a ghostly presence.

The tall man pulled in on the reins and dismounted in a thickness of firs near the edge of a meadow. He heard a sound which, at first, he believed to be the moaning of wind through the cuts and gorges of the Black Hills. The more he listened, however, the more he realized that what he was hearing was a human voice, a chanting voice. This was an Indian canticle, a deep and mysterious chant which Gunn knew was of great significance, though he couldn't understand what the Indian was saying.

Gunn tied his horse loosely to a low branch and patted him to soothe the restless animal, then he crept forward until he found the source of the song. He crouched to observe the singer.

Except for one lone pine, razed by a long-ago storm, the area was bare. Stone Legs stood two strides from the tree, his arms flung outward. The brave's voice echoed from the surrounding hills with a reverberation that struck to the soul.

Aside from a breech clout, and a red cloth which was draped across his shoulders, the Indian was naked, his bronzed body oiled, shining in the sun. Stone Legs's coarse black hair was unbound, and hanging down his back. One end of the red cloth was staked to the ground.

Gunn had heard of the elite warrior society. He knew that Stone Legs had just made a vow to Wakantanka to fight to the death, not to leave the place where he was now staked out until either he, or his enemy, was dead.

Gunn scanned the area. Large trees surrounded the sloping, grassy field. A small stream bubbled at the foot of the rise.

Out of the corner of his eye, he spotted a flutter of brush, no . . . cloth. A young woman, slim, rumpled and beautiful, stood tied to a sapling a short distance back from the rim of the basin. It was June Bixby.

A brave squatted near the girl, staring at his leader. The brave said something, and Stone Legs stopped in mid-chant, then looked toward Gunn.

"You are the man who has been following me?"

"Yes," Gunn said.

"I will finish my song," Stone Legs said. "Then we will have a good fight. First, I will sing to Wakantanka, the Great Spirit, in words that he can understand. Then, I will say to you, in English, the words I am saying to Wakantanka."

Stone Legs began chanting again, ". . . *Hun-hun-he! Hun-hun-he!*" The words rolled like thunder echoing from the Black Hills. Stone Legs did a little dance around the red sash, then finally he stopped his dance and looked at Gunn.

"It is a good day to die," he said. "All the things of my life are around me. My life is full."

"Neither of us has to die," Gunn said. "Give me the girl and I will leave."

"You would deny me the right to fight you?"

Gunn sighed. "If we must fight, we must fight," he said.

"Did you kill Broken Hand?"

"Yes."

"Was it a good fight?"

"It was a good fight," Gunn said.

"How are you called?"

"I am called Gunn."

"Ah, yes, Gunn," Stone Legs said. "It is a good name for a warrior." Stone Legs looked over at Yellow Nose. "Yellow Nose, hear me," he said. "If I am killed by this man, Gunn, he will have my red cloth. He will be a member of the Strong Hearts society. You will bear witness to my words." Stone Legs looked at Gunn. "If you kill me, you will let

Yellow Nose live?"

"Yes," Gunn said. "You would honor me by making me a member of the Strong Hearts." He looked at the girl. "Now, I ask a gift from you. If we have a good fight and I am killed, will you let the girl go?"

Stone Legs looked toward the girl, then nodded his head at Yellow Nose. Yellow Nose walked over to the girl and pulled his knife. The girl flinched in fear, until she saw that he was using his knife to cut her bonds.

"The girl is free," Stone Legs said. "Now, we will fight?"

"We will fight," Gunn agreed and he slipped the buckle of his gun belt loose, letting the weapons fall into the short grass.

Stone Legs chose the lance as his weapon. It was longer than a knife, and would have put him at an advantage over Gunn, had he not been pinned to the ground with his warrior's shawl. Stone Legs was limited as to where he could go, or what he could do, whereas Gunn, who was not pinned to the ground, could make any movement he wished. He could even run away.

Holding his knife low, Gunn danced in toward Stone Legs, then began circling around him. Stone Legs had no choice but to turn in a circle. Once or twice, Stone Legs would thrust out with his lance, stopping Gunn's progression, making him turn and begin to circle in the opposite direction.

"In your camp, there is another woman," Stone Legs said. "After I have killed you, you will see me lie with the woman that is in your camp. Your severed head will be hanging from my lodgepole, and I will prop your eyes open so that you will see everything." He made another jab with the lance, and Gunn slid away like a gliding cougar.

June stood quietly on the side, rubbing her wrists. They still hurt from the rawhide thongs which had kept her bound since she was taken prisoner. She watched the fight in fear, not fully understanding the arrangement Gunn had made with Stone Legs. She didn't know that she would be free, regardless of the outcome.

Stone Legs made another lunge toward Gunn. The white man leaned to the side, held his ground. As Stone Legs was trying to recover, Gunn cuffed him on the back of the head, sending him sprawling, face down, in the dirt. Gunn rushed to take advantage of the situation, and it was very nearly the last thing he ever did. Stone Legs rolled over quickly and slashed at Gunn with his lance. Gunn dodged the wicked point of the spear, but the lance caught his knife hand, and sent his blade flying.

Stone Legs leaped to his feet, and when Gunn started toward his knife, Stone Legs raised his lance and Gunn knew that before he could reach his weapon, the Indian could bring him down.

Gunn had no choice now but to continue the fight, unarmed. He turned back toward Stone Legs, standing with his arms spread out, dancing lightly on the balls of his feet, while Stone Legs jabbed at him, trying to finish the fight. Now Gunn's only advantage was the fact that Stone Legs was still pegged to the ground so that Gunn could avoid the thrusts by leaping backward, and Stone Legs couldn't follow through.

Gunn danced back and forth, watching the Indian's eyes, until he learned to read Stone Legs's moves. Stone Legs would flick, ever so slightly, to the left, then he would thrust right, or he would barely glance to the right, then he would thrust left. Whether it was a conscious or unconscious move on Stone Legs's part to disguise his real intentions, Gunn didn't know, but he did it four times in a row. Gunn got set, and when Stone Legs looked to the left, Gunn leaped to the left. He guessed correctly, because Stone Legs made a long lunge to the right.

With Stone Legs extended to the right, Gunn hit the ground and rolled twice until he was at his knife. Stone Legs, realizing then that he had been outsmarted, let out a yell and threw his lance. At almost the same time, Gunn sent his knife toward Stone Legs, throwing it with a snap of the wrist.

Stone Legs's lance stabbed into the ground inches away from where Gunn was lying. Gunn's throw was more accurate. It turned over, flashing once in the sun, then buried itself in Stone Legs's chest. The impact of the knife knocked Stone Legs to his knees, and he knelt there, looking down in surprise at the knife which was buried halfway to the hilt in his chest.

Gunn stood up and looked at the Indian as Stone Legs struggled to stand back up. Stone Legs pulled the bloody knife out of his chest, and as he did so, blood spewed like a fountain from his wound. Stone Legs held the knife over his head and looked up.

"Haun-nn!" Stone Legs shouted. *"Hiye haya!"* He looked at Gunn, then managed a smile. "I have told Wakantanka that I was killed by a good man," he

said. "It is a good day to die."

Stone Legs fell to his knees, then pitched forward on his face. Gunn walked over to kneel beside him, and put his hand on Stone Legs's neck to feel for a pulse. Stone Legs was dead.

"Mister," a small voice called.

Gunn looked over toward the girl, then he looked around for the other Indian.

"Where's the other one?" Gunn asked. "Where's Yellow Nose?"

"Gone," June Bixby replied. "He took off when that one went down."

"I don't like that," Gunn said. "It makes me think he may not want to live up to the bargain Stone Legs made. I think we'd better get out of here."

"That's fine by me," June said. "I want to get as far away from this place as we can."

"Are you all right?" Gunn asked. "Can you travel?"

"I'm tired and dirty, but I'm all right," she answered. "Please, let's just get out of here."

Gunn knew that they were not out of danger. As long as they stayed in these sacred hills, they were the enemy of the Sioux.

He had killed two of their bravest warriors.

Now, he thought, the Sioux would come hunting.

Hunting for him.

Chapter Thirteen

Gunn cut a new trail. Despite his agreement with Stone Legs, he was certain that Yellow Nose was going for help. If so, Yellow Nose would most certainly try and set up an ambush on Gunn's back trail. Yellow Nose took the horses when he left, so it was necessary for them to ride double on Esquire. He hoped that this roundabout route would throw off Yellow Nose, but it was taking a lot longer than he wished to get back to the valley where he had told the Bixbys to wait for him. For two hours, he had ridden a zigzag course, doubling back to see if he was being followed. He had seen no sign of pony tracks on the new trail.

By the time Gunn had returned to his own back-trail, the sun was low in the western sky. Its heat and brilliance had dissipated during its descent, and it was now a glowing red orb above the distant peaks.

June said little during the day, but Gunn was very aware of her. She sat behind him, her arms wrapped around his waist, her breasts pressing into his back. He was acutely aware of the incessant pressure of those breasts during the day, wondered how she must feel, for her nipples were taut, hard as acorns, and he was half-maddened by the sensation. Yet to acknowledge his desire would be to stir flames that were best left banked. She was, after all, a very young woman, Deanne's daughter, and a girl for whom he now had a responsibility.

He turned his head, spoke over his shoulder.

"Yellow Nose might bring a war party after us yet, and I'd like to avoid that if I can. I want to make it as tough for him as I can. It may take a little longer, but we'll get back to your folks soon. Don't be afraid."

"I'm not afraid," June said, and her voice showed him that she was, indeed, a courageous girl.

"Hang on," he muttered and as June tightened her grip around his waist, he gently nudged Esquire down the slope of a steep gully.

The big Walker sat back on his haunches and gingerly descended through the loose rocks and bushy squirreltail grass which was growing in the gully.

The light faded, shadowed the floor of the wash.

Gunn pulled back on the reins and brought the horse to a halt before a black hole on the gully wall. He helped the girl swing down and dismounted.

"We may as well stop here for the night," he said. "Here's enough of a cave to give us a place to stay."

June stood aside, watching quietly as the big man unsaddled and brushed Esquire down with a currying brush he kept in his saddlebag. Finally she spoke.

"You brush your horse down, even out here?"

"Especially out here," Gunn said. "Esquire's worked hard, he deserves to be well treated. After all, he doesn't know what kind of trouble we're in. He just knows to do his best."

"He's a good horse," June said.

Gunn smiled and turned to her.

"Yes. You'd better stretch your legs, June. And gather some firewood. We can boil some coffee back in that hole. The fire will be far enough in so as not to attract attention."

June Bixby stepped into the growing darkness and stooped to pick up sticks and branches of fallen wood. She returned and dropped the wood on the floor of the cave. She was quiet while Gunn built the fire, reflective while the coffee boiled. Finally the coffee's aroma filled the inside of the cave, and Gunn poured a cup.

"You all right?" Gunn asked.

She nodded, her head casting a moving shadow on the firelighted wall. He handed her a cup of hot, black coffee, dug jerky and hardtack out of his saddlebag.

"It's not much," he said. "Keep your stomach from growling all night."

"This is fine. I'm not very hungry."

They chewed, washed the dry food down with coffee. Gunn welcomed the silence. The dark had come on and he felt safe in the cave. He poured more coffee in both cups, looked at the girl as she stared pensively into the fire.

"Were they rough on you?" he asked.

A sob broke in the girl's throat.

"They knocked me around some and tied my hands. The one you called Stone Legs led me by a leather strap around my neck." Her hand went to her neck as if to rub away the memory of the thong.

"Here. Let me have a look at that." The man

moved close to the girl and gently pulled back her collar. A raw crease rimmed her neck.

"Loosen your collar. I'll get some cool water to bathe it."

The girl unfastened the top buttons on her dress and drew back the fabric. Her creamy skin glowed in the flicker of the campfire.

Gunn returned to her side and dabbed at the wound with a wet neckerchief.

The silent girl watched the top of his dark head as he worked on the cut. She set the cup of hot liquid aside and raised one hand, placed her fingers along his cheek.

"You're a very gentle man."

The movement and soft words startled Gunn. He drew back to look into the clear, blue eyes.

Her other hand came up, cupped his other cheek. She leaned her face toward him and gently kissed his lips.

He placed his hands atop hers and drew them slowly from his face.

"June," he husked. "Time to rest. We've got a long ride ahead of us tomorrow."

The girl nodded and lay back on the blanket he had spread for her.

"Where will you sleep?" she asked.

"I'll prop against the saddle," he replied.

"Please sleep next to me," she begged. "I'm so afraid out here. Those Indians . . ." Tears welled in her eyes. Her voice broke as she fought down the rising hysteria. Gunn saw that she was going through a kind of delayed shock. He had seen it happen. A person could be cool and level-headed under pressure, but when the danger was over, some collapsed, turned to jelly.

Without a word, the man moved the saddle next to the girl's bedding and sat leaning against the smooth leather.

The fire sputtered and died to red embers as the guardian and his charge nodded to sleep in the lonesome pit along the wash.

Sometime later, he awoke suddenly, and felt hands rubbing, caressing his thighs.

"June?"

"Gunn," she whispered and continued to stroke his legs, her hands hot through the denim.

He straightened himself against the saddle, tried to remove her hands. Her pale face floated in front of him, the blue eyes bright, shining in the fading firelight. Her smooth, young body glowed in silhouette as she sat naked before him.

"June." This time his voice was firm, paternal. "June, this is no good for either of us. You just stir up things best left to lie."

She leaned back on her heels, her long, black hair loose around her white shoulders.

"I want you, Mister Gunn. I'm burning inside. Ever since . . . since you came and found me . . ."

"You're still in shock," he said. "It happens. Maybe grateful. You don't owe me anything."

"It's not that. I want you. Please don't torture me. Take me, Gunn. Make love to me."

"No, I can't do that." He held her hands now, the feel of them still hot on his thighs.

She moved toward him, pressed her small, upturned breasts into his chest, the same breasts he had felt against his back all day, only now they were bare, hot, smooth, and tipped by hard little nipples. June kissed him full on the lips.

"June, no," he said. Despite his best intentions, he felt himself reacting to her.

"Maybe I am grateful. You saved me, Mister Gunn. I want to repay you."

"You don't have to repay me like that," Gunn said. "I'm not asking you to do anything like that."

"I know I don't have to, Mister Gunn, but I want to. I've been thinking about it all day . . . about you, and about what it would be like. I'm hot . . . all hot inside."

She unfastened the buttons on his shirt, leaned against him again and squirmed hard into his chest.

"June, you'll hate yourself. Stop. Stop now, and there'll be no harm done."

"I can't stop it . . . and neither can you." She reached for him, for the growing hardness that pressed against the denim of his trousers. She caressed his cock through the fabric, caused him to moan with the motion.

Her breasts rubbed against his partially bare chest as her fingers worked to unbutton his pants.

He found himself responding, helping her with the fasteners.

The two lay naked together in the coolness of the cave.

He leaned down, kissed her on the mouth.

"Oh, yes, Gunn," she moaned, parting her lips to welcome his tongue.

Her tongue responded to his, slithered into his wet mouth, explored, searched.

"You sure about this?" Gunn murmured, his voice cracked with emotion.

"Yes, oh, yes," she responded and slid her hand down to grasp his swollen manhood. She kneaded it, massaged it gently. The shaft filled with blood and throbbed, stiffened more.

Gunn knew there was no stopping now. The girl knew what she wanted and now he wanted it too, so he responded. He leaned across her, kissed her breasts. His tongue flicked at the nipples, circled them, teased them. Drawing one firm breast into his mouth, he suckled deeply.

She groaned, writhed with pleasure.

"Now, Gunn. I want you now. Deep inside me," she breathed. Her blue eyes sparkled in the dying light.

He moved above her, gazed down at her young beauty. Her budding breasts were tender mounds that heaved gently with her every breath. Her black hair glistened like the blue-black of a raven's wing.

She opened her legs to him, offering the dark thatch, the pink gash of her womanhood. He moved down and she rose to meet him as he entered her, parted the moist, swollen lips and drove into her steaming flesh.

The girl trembled as the stalk slid into her hidden place, quivered with pleasure.

His stroke was shallow, gently meeting the tender barrier of her virginity. He repeated the smooth, restrained plunge, each time meeting the obstacle to his fulfillment.

"Please," she said. "All the way. I want you to go

all the way."

A moan of ecstasy rose from the girl as a final stab freed the barrier and sent the shaft to her depths.

"Oh, Gunn," she moaned. "I can feel you inside of me. Deeper, please, deeper."

He gave in to her demand, held tight to her twisting writhing body as he thrust deep inside her. Her hands flailed at his back, caressed, kneaded. Her hips moved in rhythm with his own, slowly at first, then faster, harder.

A rolling moan rose from deep in her throat as the first rush of orgasm claimed her. She bucked with the suddenness of the pleasure. She held fast to him as the orgasm passed over her. He drew long strokes as his shaft passed over the trigger of her passion. June bucked again. Held tight to him.

"Yes, yes," she moaned. "That's what I wanted. So good, Gunn. So good."

He grasped her firm buttocks in his hands, helped her rise to meet his strokes. She tilted her loins, allowed him to dive deeper into her hot cavern.

She lowered her eyes and could see the shaft moving in and out of her tunnel, feel its power and thickness. A shock wave of pleasure swept over her again as she tried to hurry, to devour, to be filled.

He rose and fell faster now, heard her sobs, her moans of rapture as the orgasms almost consumed her.

Gunn's body was oiled with sweat as he rammed deep, stroked fast.

"Forever, Gunn. I could do this forever," June murmured.

But forever was too long for Gunn to wait. He felt

his own juices leap, boil. Pleasure ran like a copper wire through his body, a charge of ignited gunpowder running to every nerve, every pore.

A low scream rose in her throat as she clutched him, dug her fingers into his flesh. Her voice reached a high-pitched wail and he let go.

His rush of seed hurled itself from his body in the pain and pleasure of the moment and rushed into the depths of her hot valley.

He kissed her gently and rolled from her heated body into the cool air of the cave.

"Thank you, Gunn," she whispered. "Thank you for so much."

His breathing slowed as he took her in his arms and pulled the blanket around their nakedness.

The two slept entwined.

The steel-colored eyes flashed open. Gunn lay still, listened.

The dry rattle of brush outside the mouth of the little cave slashed through his drowsiness.

He glanced at the sleeping girl. Then silently he pulled on his pants, shook out his boots and slid them on. With one hand on the Winchester '73, he crept to the opening, listened.

The harsh, rasping noise came again from out of the blackness.

Gunn crouched, moved in the direction of the sound. Sweat gathered on his face. Again he heard the sound. Something . . . or someone brushed against foliage.

He reached the rocks at the bottom of the arroyo

and stopped.

The bulky shape of a horse stood against the far side of the wash. He took a deep breath and prowled toward the lone animal.

Another sound from under a low fir tree stopped the tall man in his tracks. The new sound was soft, steady, like a child snoring.

Gunn stepped to the side of the standing horse and patted it gently, calmed it. He edged silently to the sleeping bundle by the tree and knelt down, his rifle steady in his hand.

The barrel of the gun nudged the rounded form.

"Hey, you," he called quietly and prodded the form.

The bundle emitted a small yip and sat erect.

Deanne Bixby stared up at him.

Chapter Fourteen

"Gunn!" Deanne said. "Oh, Gunn, it's you! I found you!"

"Where's your husband?"

"He wouldn't come with me, so I left him," she said. "I . . . I couldn't stay there any more and watch him go crazy over gold while all the time June was a prisoner of the Indians, might even be dead for all we know."

"June is safe," Gunn said.

"She's safe? How do you know? Have you seen her? Do you know where she is?"

"She's with me," Gunn said. "We're in a cave just up a way."

"I want to see her," Deanne said.

"Give me your horse . . . I'll put her with Esquire."

Gunn pointed out the way to the cave, while he took Deanne's mare over to tether with Esquire. When he got back a few moments later, he saw that the embers of last night's campfire had been rekindled, and the flames were now casting a soft, golden light on the walls of the cave. Deanne was standing there with a look of shock on her face, while June was trying, unsuccessfully, to cover her nude body with the saddle blanket.

Pat Bixby awoke to the rank smell of his own body. He had a bad taste in his mouth, and his head was hurting. On a nearby rock he saw the smashed remains of an empty whiskey bottle, and he remembered now that he had drunk himself to sleep last night. Now the sun was high and hot above him.

The heavy man rose unsteadily, touched the side of his throbbing head. Too much whiskey, too many hours stooped in the glaring hot stream and too little sleep caught up with the unfit man.

"Deanne," he muttered to himself. "Where are you?" His tongue was thick, his tone whined. The wind fluttered through the canopy of leaves above his head. He realized then that Deanne was gone, had left him yesterday. That was one of the reasons he had drunk himself into insensibility last night.

Bixby dragged his heels across to the hard-packed fire circle and began boiling some coffee.

"You shouldn't have left me, Deanne. I'd of been ready soon. Got enough gold now to start over somewhere." The red-rimmed eyes filled with moisture. He wiped his sleeve across his nose.

"I want June back as much as you. But the gold was so close," he continued, talking to himself.

"Goddamnit, Deanne! Where are you?" he yelled at the hills. His echo bounced back at him. Then faded to an empty, mocking silence.

Pat Bixby found himself on the verge of panic. His mind envisioned Deanne and June helpless in the hands of the savages. The only two people who meant anything to him might be tortured—or worse.

A croaking sound broke in Bixby's throat, tears streamed down his puffy cheeks. He wiped his face with his sleeve and plodded toward the horses.

He saddled his horse and prepared the pack mule for the trip. The lone, unarmed man headed north, following the trail of his wife, Gunn, and the Brules who held his daughter captive.

Dark clouds rolled up from the western horizon. A crash of thunder rumbled across the hills. A drop of rain splashed against the back of his hand.

He gazed up at the sky and swore. A storm might make his search difficult, if not impossible. No matter, he wouldn't stop, not until he found Deanne and June.

The trail turned into a slippery, mossy ribbon of mud. Charcoal Calf leaped down from his pony and inspected the track. A sliver of stone was missing from the small rock in his hand. Struck by a metal shoe. The strike was fresh, a white scar on stone.

The brave raised his arm and swung the rifle in a slow arc above his head.

Hoofbeats slogged through the mud, headed toward the young Indian.

Three Brules swung onto the path, joined the youth.

"Here," he nodded and grabbed the mane of his paint. He swung onto the horse's back and turned to face his companions.

"The tall man follows this path. He has killed

Broken Hand and Stone Legs. But now I will kill him! *Hu kah hay!*" he shouted, and kicked the belly of his horse. The three fell in behind the angry young brave, followed him up the slope.

Rain slashed at the man and the two women. They were soaked to the skin, cold in the sudden storm. The blankets that wrapped the Bixby women lay heavy with moisture, dripped water down the sides of the tired horses. June Bixby rested her head against the man's soaked back.

The tall man studied the steep trail, blinked his eyes against the stinging lash of the raindrops. He fought the veil of water as he searched for shelter.

In a break of lightning flash, he saw a rock overhang which had been dug by centuries of wind and rushing water. It was shallow, but it did offer shelter from the driving force of the rain. He glanced back at Deanne Bixby, her head bowed to the pelting water.

"Over here!" he shouted into the storm. "Hey! Over here!"

The woman saw him, followed his lead.

Gunn reached the hollow first, the height allowing him to stay mounted.

"Stay on your horse," he commanded. "We'll rest a few minutes, wait until it slacks up a bit."

The woman nodded her obedience and bowed her head against the wind.

"Sonovabitch! He's gone!" Fred Wykoff kicked at a stone that sat in the blackened fire circle.

"I saw him lying here until long past sun up.

Thought that the time was right to come in and get the gold," Gorman stated. "He must have moved out as the storm was blowing in."

"Well, we know he didn't come our way. We had the south ridge sewed up. He must have moved on north," Maxwell Lee added.

"Come on!" Gorman shouted. "He can't be too far ahead of us. This rain will slow him down. That means he'll stay on the trail. It'll be easy to find him."

The three men turned their horses north, followed Pat Bixby's muddy trail.

Gunn and June Bixby sat still atop the Tennessee Walker, listened to the torrents. Gunn had intended to stay only a few moments, until the rain slackened, but the rain was showing no signs of let-up. He realized then that he shouldn't stay here much longer. They would have to go back out into the rain. He took a deep breath, then shouted at the women.

"Come on, we've got to get out of here," he said. "It's not safe. This is a natural wash. A flash flood could pour down on us at any time." He leaned across his horse and grabbed the older woman's reins. "Here," he said, grasping them in his hand. "You hold on to the saddle horn and give me these. We've got to get to higher ground."

The big sorrel reluctantly moved out into the gray sheet of water, nudged onward by his rider. The small caravan stepped its way precariously along a narrow ledge that led from the base of the wash across the top of the outcrop that had been their safe harbor.

Behind them, they could hear a crashing thunder

which sounded like the roar of fifty locomotives as the flash flood Gunn had worried about began to rush through the gully. Gunn prodded Esquire up the ledge, pulled forcefully on the reins of the following horse to tug Deanne's mare up also.

Lightning slashed the air as Gunn turned to look down into the gully. A river of brown, boiling water rushed below them in a deadly rising tide. The flood swept toward them, swirling high, filling the wash.

He spoke softly, calmly to Esquire, continued to prod him upward to the rim. The front hoof of the sorrel gained the lip of the ridge as the murky water swirled about the feet of the Bixby woman's mare. The timid horse lurched, panicked.

Esquire topped the rim as Gunn tugged on the reins of the following horse, tried to calm her. Deanne Bixby screamed as the horse reared, attempted to back down the trail. Gunn gripped the leather reins until they cut his hands. June Bixby tightened her arms around the man's waist, almost cut off his air. He jerked at the mare's head, got her attention. The animal settled down and pulled herself over the rim, just as the water spilled over the top of the gully. Had they still been down in the gully, they would have been washed away, drowned like rats in a cellar.

Gunn handed the reins back to Deanne, then pushed his horse upslope toward a grove of pines. He spotted a likely place of cover under the branches where a big tree had fallen, leaving a tangle of roots and a natural pit. He worked quickly to pull boughs over the roof of gnarled branches and hobbled the horses under a low, bushy juniper.

The drenched threesome squatted under the canopy of thick pines for a few moments, then Gunn edged his way to the opening of the muddy pit, flexed his leather-burned hand in the cooling rain and looked around.

Jagged sheets of lightning split the air, followed almost immediately by a crash of thunder. The lightning flash was so close that the air smelled of ozone.

Gunn saw movement on the facing wall above the trail. He waited and stared. A black head and bronze face appeared from behind a boulder.

Brules.

Gunn knew it now. They had not given up. He knew all along they wouldn't.

He sat there for another moment, then turned to the women.

"Might as well let you know where we stand," he said above the storm. "I saw Indians out there. Not more than three or four. But they're out there."

"Charcoal Calf," Deanne said.

Gunn looked toward her.

"Charcoal Calf escaped night before last. He took Pat's weapons. Gunn, he's looking for you. He wants to kill you."

"Yeah. No surprise there," Gunn said. He moved back into the shelter and squatted there, watching the rain sweep across the space in front of them.

"I . . . I'm sorry," Deanne finally said. "I had no right to be angry. It's just that, when I saw my daughter naked last night, I . . ."

"Mama, I asked him," June said. "It was my doing. I . . . I begged him."

"June!"

"I couldn't help myself," June said. "You don't

know what I'd been through. You don't know how much I . . . needed him."

Deanne sighed, and took her daughter's hand. "Maybe I do know," she said. "Anyway, I'm sorry I got angry, and I beg you to forgive me."

"There's nothing to forgive," June said.

Gunn said nothing. This was between mother and daughter, and though he realized that he was the subject of their discussion, he was not comfortable joining in. He inched forward again and looked out through the opening, as much to get away from their conversation, as to see what was going on.

The rain continued throughout the rest of the day so there was no sunset visible, merely a gradual lessening of gray light. Finally all the light was gone and Gunn knew they were going to have to spend the night here, in this improvised shelter.

"I'm hungry," June said. "What I wouldn't give for a good, thick stew, and some biscuits, dripping with butter."

"And afterward, a big piece of apple pie," Deanne offered.

"And milk," Gunn added.

Deanne laughed.

"Are we ever going to have any of those things again, Gunn?" she asked. "Are we ever going to get out of here?"

"Yeah," Gunn said. "We're going to get out of here." The women were sitting, one to each side of him, and they leaned against him for comfort and warmth. They stayed that way for a long time, then,

Gunn heard June's soft, rhythmic breathing.

"Is she asleep?" Deanne asked.

"Yes."

"I'm glad. She's had quite a bad time of it. She needs her sleep."

"Yes," Gunn agreed.

"I'm sorry I got angry last night when I saw June naked. It's just that, it didn't take me long to figure out what happened, and when I figured it out, well, I just got angry, that's all."

"That's all right," Gunn said.

Deanne sighed. "No, it's not all right. I guess the reason I got so angry was because I had no right to get angry," she said. "What can I say to her when she has done no more than I have already done? What is there about you, Gunn? What is there about you that makes women behave in such a way?"

"Hush," Gunn said softly. "You need to get some sleep too. I promised you and June I'd get you out of here, but I can only do that if you're both rested enough to help yourself."

"All right," Deanne said. "I'll get some sleep."

He looked at the women, wondered if he could make good on his promise.

Charcoal Calf looked at the three who rode with him. He had told them of his vision of Broken Hand, and that vision had made him a chieftain in their eyes. They were now ready to follow him, and they believed he would lead them to a glorious victory. Charcoal Calf sang a song for them.

In this circle, hear what I sing
I am a Brule,
I am prepared to die.
When one knows of life,
Already there is death.
When one knows of danger,
Already there is courage.
When there is before,
Already there is after.
I am a Brule.
I am prepared to die.
In this circle, hear what I sing.

Charcoal Calf finished his song, then looked around the boulder at the place where he knew Gunn and the women were hiding. He smiled. Soon, Broken Hand would be avenged.

Chapter Fifteen

The man called Gunn awakened slowly to a dull throb in his legs and arms. With his eyes closed, he remained motionless while he collected his bearings. He felt the weight, the warmth of the two women who leaned against him for comfort and protection.

"Gunn?"

At the sound of Deanne's murmur, he opened his eyes to the gray light of early dawn.

"Yeah?" he croaked.

"I heard something out there," she breathed.

"Wait here. I'll check," he responded in a hoarse whisper. He leaned the still-sleeping June against the side of the earthen cave and eased forward on stiffened limbs.

At the edge of the pit he waited, adjusted his vision to the growing light. In the rain, and in the feeble light of the evening before, he had not been able to see clearly enough to establish their exact location. They had taken shelter in the pit formed by the falling tree out of desperation, not by design. A fine mist was still falling. But despite the mist, he was able to see more clearly now, make out the definitions of the terrain.

He saw the trail. It followed a natural wash through the saddleback between two hills. Though the upper, more gentle slopes of the hills were covered with the dark fir trees which gave the hills their name, the lower slopes steepened, and the gully through which the trail passed was flanked by striated cliffs, eroded and the silt redeposited by the flow of ancient waters. The erosion action had also left bands of vari-colored sediment from the runoff of surrounding hills. He could see the ruddy ochre of iron, the faint yellow of sulphur.

He gazed at the far side of the trail, caught movement among the low growth.

A Brule, legs and arms spread out like a stalking spider, crept along the downside of the slope. The Indian kept his head down, moving with stealth, in slow motion. A careless eye would not have seen the tedious labor nor the concealed form of the Indian. The bronze skin and tanned breech cloth melded with the color of the earth. His movement was slow and studied, much like the slow, mechanical motion of a walking stick.

Gunn reached for the Winchester.

He spoke over his shoulder to his companion.

"You better wake June," he said. "If I have to shoot, I don't want her to wake up screaming. Don't make any noise."

Then he moved the long, blued barrel of the Winchester into position, balanced the figure of the Brule in his front and rear sights. He drew a breath, held it, as his finger curled around the trigger.

Holding steady on his target, Gunn slowly

squeezed the thin chunk of metal in one smooth motion.

Pat Bixby's sleeping frame jolted upright. The movement slammed his head into the low overhang of rock.

"Damnit," he muttered, rubbing his head. The cause of the sound that startled the fat man finally sank into his brain as he looked around the cave where he had taken shelter the night before.

"Gunshot," he said and eased close to the yawning mouth of the dank cave.

Another shot rang out from the trail up ahead. Bixby peered around the rocks to catch a glimpse of the action.

The body of an Indian lay sprawled across the path. Another slumped forward over a boulder a little farther up the hillside.

"Gunn? That you up there?" the fat man shouted.

"Yeah!" came the reply. "Keep your head down, Bixby. There's two more Indians up there. Just lay low until this is over."

"You find June?"

"She's here. And so is Deanne. Now stay down."

"All right," Pat replied and scooted back to the depths of the shallow cave.

"You hear that, Gorman?" Fred Wykoff asked.

"I heard."

"Looks like Gunn is pinned down. He oughta stay busy for awhile. We can pick off the fat man, take his gold and light a shuck before anyone's the wiser."

"That's what it looks like to me," Gorman replied, in a tone of voice that made it plain he was still in charge. "But, listen to me. We gotta do it right and we gotta do it quick. Can you see Bixby?"

"No, but I know where he is. He's in that cave over yonder." Wykoff aimed the rifle toward the maw of the cave and squeezed off a shot.

The bullet pinged against the rock and ricocheted into the dirt inches away from Bixby's reclining body. He levered another round into the chamber, raised his sights and fired again. The bullet entered the cave, slammed against the rock wall, then ricocheted with a loud whine, spanging off stone, the sound echoing long after the bullet was spent.

"Goddamnit, Gunn. Somebody is shooting at me!" the frightened man shouted.

"I heard," Gunn replied. "Now shut up and lay low."

Bixby flattened his bulk against the back side of the shadowed niche.

Gunn turned to Deanne. "Can you handle one of these?" he asked, tapping the stock of the rifle.

She nodded. He handed the rifle to her. She took it without a word.

"Now listen to me," he said. "Those hardcases that are after the gold are out there and have your husband pinned down in a cave. I'm going to work my way across from them and see if I can't run them off. You sit here back from the opening and watch that boulder across there. There's two Brules back of it. Don't shoot until you've got a clear target." He paused. "Can you handle it?"

"I can handle it," she breathed.

"Good. Just remember what I told you."

Deanne nodded again as the big man eased one of his hand guns out of its holster and darted out of the pit. An orange blossom of rifle fire flared from the boulder across the trail. The bullet slashed into the pine boughs over the woman's head, sent splinters raining down on her damp shoulders. She squinted across the sights of the barrel, but saw no target.

Gunn ran a zigzag pattern across the dark wooded slope and slid under the outspread arms of a low-limbed juniper. He sat above Bixby's shelter and back several yards from the overhang that sheltered it.

A horse stamped somewhere across the slope and voices floated in muttered whispers on the morning mist. He strained to see, to pinpoint the sounds, but he saw nothing and the sounds blurred like the mist itself.

The tall man took up a handful of pebbles and bowled them across the rock shelf above Bixby's head.

The stones scattered off the lip of the ledge, sprinkled to the mud in front of the covering fat man huddled in the cave.

"Bixby," Gunn blurted, his voice low.

"Yeah," came the response.

"You got a rifle?"

"Nope. The Injun boy stole all our weapons," he replied.

"You see those firs off to your left?"

"Yep."

"When I lay down a cover of fire, you haul your butt into those trees."

"But, Gunn . . ."

"Do it!" Gunn commanded. "Now!" he shouted and emptied all six chambers of the .44 into the opposite hillside.

The fat man gained his feet and half-ran, half-crawled up the slope to the dark trees. He rolled under the boughs of a leaning pine. His barrel chest heaved from the burst of exercise. One fleshy hand reached for the bulge that lay heavy under his shirt. The skin bag was tied tight around his neck with a leather thong.

"Did you see where he went?" Maxwell Lee asked his companions.

"Well, now what do you think, Lee? Sure, I had my head up the whole time those bullets were coming in on us," Lucas Gorman growled. "No, you dunce, I didn't see where he went." Gorman's anger made his eyes bulge, his neck puff up like an adder's. "Let's get this over with," he added.

"You got any suggestions?" Wykoff asked.

"It appears to me that we've got some Indians to contend with now. Bixby's got no weapon or else he would have shot at us. Lee, you edge over there toward them Injuns. I'm going to work my way down to Bixby's mule. The gold might be on that pack animal. Wykoff, you keep Gunn off our backs."

"What about the women?" Wykoff asked.

"Well, what about 'em?"

"We just gonna leave 'em there?"

"There'll be time for them when this is over, you randy buck," Gorman snapped. "We got Gunn and the Injuns to deal with and you just thinkin' about where to stick your pecker." He took a long breath, let it out, and fixed Wykoff with a scathing look.

"Just forget about the damned women."

"I was just askin' is all."

"Shit," said Gorman, "just keep your damned mind on business." He crouched, then, and disappeared into the underbrush.

"Lay down some cover!" Lee shouted and darted upslope.

Wykoff clipped off shots around the brushy juniper at regular intervals until Lee disappeared in the second growth brush near the Indians.

Gunn lay, chin in the dirt and reloaded the pistol. He watched the man head toward the boulder then disappear into the trees. He didn't recognize the crouched man who crabbed through the brush. A movement down the trail flashed in the corner of Gunn's eye. Gunn shifted his gaze, watched Gorman slide down the steep slope and dart across the trail in the direction of Bixby's mule. If the man was trying to escape, he'd cause no further trouble. So it was Wykoff who had him pinned down.

"Wykoff!" he shouted. "What do you want?"

The hardcase paused at the call of his name, then spoke. "Ha! Gunn! Didn't think you'd remember me."

"What do you want?" Gunn repeated.

"Well, now, what do you think we want? Bixby's gold. And we're going to get it!" Wykoff yelled, and squeezed off a shot into the dark evergreen.

The bullet whined past Gunn's head, burned the air, and glanced off a rock somewhere on the hill.

Gunn rolled a body width closer to the base of the bush and sent an answering shot toward Wykoff.

"Coming through Wykoff!" came a shout from down the trail. Gorman came up the path using Bixby's pack mule as protection. He hung to the pack, his feet a few inches from the ground.

Gunn aimed at one of Gorman's hands that gripped the pack saddle on the mule. He tightened up on the trigger and slowly took up the slack. The .44 barked. The bullet grazed the knuckles of the man's left hand, startled the mule. The animal reared, releasing Gorman's hold.

"Goddamnit!" Gorman cried and darted to the far side of the mule. The injured man led the animal into the trees on Gunn's side of the trail very near where Pat Bixby huddled in the brush, shivering with fear.

Deanne heard the action from down the trail and grew more nervous. She sat near the edge of the muddy pit with the rifle resting on her knee, her finger ready to pull the trigger. Maxwell Lee had forgotten the women holed up across from the Indians. He raised up out of the brush a few yards behind the waiting Brules, his rifle ready. It was the last careless move he ever made.

Deanne Bixby had a target. She fired, and hit it square in the chest.

Lee pitched forward like a tumbler in a circus. His body thrashed through the brush and rolled to a stop at the feet of the two savages.

"*Aaiyee!*" Charcoal Calf yelled, as much startled by the body as he was angered. The white woman had saved him from a bullet in the back. How much more shame would he have to endure before he avenged himself. The offended youth flung out his savage cry again and bounded toward the hidden Wykoff.

Deanne again sighted a target and fired at the running Indian. That shot missed its mark and whined its way to an unknown spot among the trees.

Wykoff heard the boy before he saw him and swung his rifle toward the brush. Too late. The boy fired his rifle from his hip and gut shot the startled man. Wykoff sank to his knees, both hands clasped to his fountaining belly. "Damn," he muttered and rolled onto his side, the glaze of death frosting his eyes.

Charcoal Calf ran wild with his anger. He bellowed his savage cry again and rushed down the slope, across the trail and up the hill while the startled onlookers froze in disbelief.

The boy bounded across stones, around trees and leaped to a spot near the brush where Pat Bixby lay. In a moment of courage, the fat man reached out and grabbed the brave's ankle, tripped him, causing his gun to skid across the rocky ground.

Bixby heaved his bulk from under the bush, grabbed the rifle and smashed the butt into the boy's temple.

"I got him, Gunn!" Bixby shouted.

Gorman chose that moment to draw a bead on the excited man. The shot rang out, struck the fat man in his fleshy chest. Bixby fell back as though struck full bore with a maul.

"It's just me and you, Gunn!" Gorman called out. "That other Injun lit out after Lee fell in on him."

"What are you going to do about it?" Gunn asked.

"It looks like I'm setting here between you and the women folk. And Bixby's dead. I can see him from here. He ain't moving."

A loud wail broke from the shelter of the pines and Deanne raced down the slope toward where Bixby lay.

"No, Deanne!" Gunn called. "Stay back. Gorman is up there."

The woman did not heed the warning and continued until she reached her husband's side.

"Help me, Gunn!" she shouted. "He's still alive."

"Gorman!" Gunn yelled. "Gorman?"

No answer came from the hardcase, only the fading sound of thrashing brush moving up the hillside.

Chapter Sixteen

Pat Bixby didn't move. Gunn felt his thready pulse, stood up, his face a grim mask.

"He's in a bad way, Deanne," Gunn said in a low voice.

"Oh, Pat, I'm so sorry," Deanne sobbed.

"We'd better get him back in the cave. It's the only place we have a fighting chance. Whoever is still out there will have only one way to get to us."

Deanne nodded and watched the tall man lift her bulky husband's bloody body. Gunn's muscular chest and arms strained under the weight, his legs taut in their sure movements up the rocky slope.

Pat Bixby groaned as Gunn laid him on the cool earthen floor of the cave. Blood stained the fat man's shirt in an ever-widening circle.

"I'm going back to the horses for water and blankets," Gunn said.

"June," breathed Deanne. "Bring June back with you. She's probably frightened to death up there alone."

Gunn nodded and strode from the darkness of the cave.

The sun rose to its mid-morning mark and dried up the light mist. The woods smelled of fresh earth, damp grasses. Flies swarmed around the bodies that dotted the hilly battlefield. Gunn walked upslope near the body of the boy, Charcoal Calf. He glanced down at the youth, saw his face twitch under the itch of the buzzing insects.

Gunn leaned over the youth, felt his neck. A strong pulse beat under the bronze skin.

"Don't have time to look after you now, boy," Gunn muttered and used the brave's waist thong to bind his hands and feet together. "I'll see to you later." He strode toward the pit where he had left the Bixby girl in the heat of battle.

"June," Gunn called softly at the mouth of the pit.

There was no answer.

The big man knelt and peered into the shallow darkness.

June Bixby was gone.

Gunn scanned the area, saw fresh boot tracks, the signs of a struggle. Further on, he saw her tracks mingled with another's. The story was plain to see. June had put up a good fight, but the stronger man had overcome her, shoved her in front of him.

If her captor didn't kill her right away, Gunn thought there was a good chance he might get her back. She would slow the man down. The track was easy to follow. June was spunky, he gave her that. He moved out, following the spoor as easily as if June had left messages scrawled on the trail. She had driven her boot heels in deep and they were as sharp and as clear as claim stakes.

Lucas Gorman pushed the girl ahead of him. The wet grass soaked the hem of her skirt, hung heavy about her legs.

"Come on girl, damn you. Can't you move no faster?" he asked, an impatient edge to his voice.

June Bixby shook her head and stumbled up the rocky incline. The soaked gingham swirled, twisted between her ankles, made her fall.

Gorman prodded her in the back with his rifle. "Get up, girl. We've got to find shelter before your boyfriend finds us."

The girl pulled herself up, began to stagger on. But she had broken a branch, and dug an elbow into the earth. Gorman had not noticed. She watched the earth, dislodged pebbles, small stones with the toes of her boots. When she could, she rocked back on her heels, felt them sink into the ground.

"Damnit, girl, what you doing?" Gorman snarled when she pretended to lose her balance, grabbed a large stone, pulled it from its hollow in the earth. The stone rolled a few yards, crashed to a halt in thick brush.

"I—I'm trying to hurry," she said, breathlessly. "I fell."

"Just keep going. You fall, I'll pick you up. Don't go dislodging stones."

A trace of a mocking smile played on June's lips, but she turned her head so that her captor could not see it. She did not dare look back. She had already aroused his suspicions and if Gunn were tracking them, she wanted to leave him a clear trail.

Her lungs started to burn. Her side ached. Still, Gorman prodded her on, until it seemed she had reached the limit of her endurance. She started to turn and beg him to let her rest, when she saw a slight movement a few yards away. Was it only an illusion? She was lightheaded. Were her eyes playing tricks on her? Perhaps it was only a small creature, a lizard or a chipmunk that had brushed against the low branch of a fir.

She hesitated, felt Gorman's gunbarrel press into the small of her back.

"Just as well quit lagging," he said. "Gunn ain't going to find you. Ever."

Something exploded from the dripping branches ahead of her. She jerked back as terror gripped her.

"I've already found you," Gunn said and stepped from the brush in front of June.

He lunged at the pair and with a sweep of his arm, brushed June to one side. The two men faced each other, rifles raised.

"Looks like we got us a stand off here," Gorman snorted.

Gunn took a quick step toward the hardcase and ducked low. He swung the Winchester stock into the barrel of Gorman's gun. The outlaw's rifle bellowed and sent a bullet crashing harmlessly into the upper branches of a tall blue spruce. The acrid stench of gunpowder burned Gunn's eyes as he knocked the smoking gun into the brush.

"What're you gonna do, now, Gunn?" Gorman asked. "Shoot me down in cold blood?"

"It's tempting."

"I'd like a little out of your hide first."

Gunn started to step back, when the hardcase lunged. In his desperation, he was fast.

Gorman kicked at the Winchester, caused it to drop, and arched a fist toward Gunn's jaw.

Gunn blocked the racing fist with his forearm and drove his own knotted hand into the outlaw's belly.

A gusty blast of breath exploded from Gorman's lips. He halted, flat-footed, stunned by the punch. He tried to answer with another roundhouse right, but Gunn slipped under it easily, backpedaled. Gorman, too, backed away, swaying like some wounded beast.

Gunn moved in quickly and smashed his left into the side of Gorman's head.

Blood spurted from a split ear.

Gorman roared with pain, stepped in close to try and wrestle Gunn to the ground. The tall man ducked under the clamping arms, brought his fist up from ground level and drove a right into the outlaw's heart.

Gorman swayed, fought for air then stepped in to meet a hard left to his jaw.

The hardcase flailed the air, landed a glancing blow to Gunn's cheek.

Gunn moved in close, hammered two more blows to Gorman's head.

The hardcase encircled the big man with his massive arms, caged him in a vise-like grip.

Gunn struggled, pressed his muscular arms against those of the attacker, broke the bear hold. The two staggered apart, panting. Gorman's lungs made a wheezing sound like a blacksmith's bellows. The exertion showed in the slump of his shoulders. He fought for his second wind and Gunn knew that he could not lose his advantage or he would go down. His own arms felt like leaden sashweights and he could feel his heart pumping so hard he thought it would burst from his chest.

Gunn again stepped in and drove his right wrist-deep into Gorman's flaccid belly.

The man staggered, sank to his knees near the Winchester.

Gunn saw the motion as the hardcase lifted the rifle.

He eased the Colt from its velvet smooth leather and fired down at the kneeling man. A blinding flash and deafening explosion shattered the silence, white smoke swirled about Lucas Gorman like dragon's breath.

The Winchester barked, flamed and spewed fire and lead into the ground inches from Gunn's feet.

A stain of red spread across Gorman's chest. The hardcase gurgled a pleading sound as the blood rose in his throat, dribbled from the corners of his mouth. He pitched forward, fell flat on his belly, his face slamming deep in the wet grass of the slope.

Deanne Bixby did not delude herself. Her husband was dying and her daughter was gone, taken by a killer.

Pat's breath rattled deep in his bronchials. She rubbed his forehead tenderly, gently, as though he were a child. She rocked slowly on the cool cave floor, cushioning her husband's head in her lap.

"Oh, Pat," she crooned, "why did it have to turn out like this? Why did you have to have that . . . that insane drive for the gold? What does it matter now? What good did it do you? Oh, why didn't you listen to me? Why couldn't I make you understand? I know I haven't been a very good wife for you . . . but I could have been. I would have been if you had just given me a chance."

Bixby groaned and his eyes opened wide for a moment, then closed. His lips turned blue for a moment, and a ripple of fear coursed through Deanne's stomach as if she had just fallen from a great height.

She mopped Pat's head with water from a canteen that Gunn had brought.

She fumbled through the saddle bags next to her and found the stump of a candle. She held it to a tongue of flame from the fire.

Its light flickered small and lonely in the dark cave.

The woman loosened the knot of hair at her neck, let the mass of blond strands fall and began to brush vigorously. Maybe, she thought, that would stop the shaking, the fear-tremble that threatened to shake her loose from her senses.

The crackle of a breaking branch caused the woman to stiffen with terror. She slid out from under Pat's head, stood up, then backed toward the wall.

"Deanne!" Gunn's voice called. "We're coming in."

The woman rushed toward them, her arms outstretched. Relief poured through her tense body as her daughter collapsed in her arms and began to sob. The mother held the girl tight, comforted her, stroked her hair.

"I brought someone else with me," Gunn said. "It looks like you get to look after this one for awhile longer." He pushed Charcoal Calf ahead of him into the cave. The boys hands were tied in front of him. "I'm going to gather some wood. Might find enough dry to build a little fire."

The older woman nodded and watched the bound Indian squat against the wall.

"I'm glad you weren't killed," she said.

"Why? We are enemies. I would have killed you if I had the chance."

"Don't you understand?"

"Understand what?" The Brule glared at her.

"Can you go home, boy?" she asked.

The young Brule glared at her, hatred filled his eyes.

"You saved our lives, you know," she said softly.

A puzzled look crossed the boy's face.

"That man you shot . . . Wykoff? Well, he had Gunn pinned down and would've killed me if he got the chance."

Charcoal Calf looked hard at the woman, the pinched glaze of loathing faded from his eyes.

"I'll tell Gunn when he gets back. Maybe he'll let you loose. He's a good man. He doesn't kill folks unless they need killing."

The woman sat silent for a time and rocked her husband.

June lay against the cave wall, staring straight into the fire as though she was in shock. Her shoulders slumped and her breath was shallow.

The Indian boy relaxed against the wall of the cave, his face in shadow.

"This cave," the boy said. "This is a place of ghosts."

The woman jumped slightly, startled at the sound of the boy's voice.

"My father and his father tell of the Old Ones, the Ones Who Walked Before. They were the people from whom all other people come," he continued.

"The Old Ones could rise up into the air and soar above the peaks. It is said that some of them live in these hills even now. This is the holy road. The sacred hills."

Deanne watched the boy and nodded at his words.

"I have seen fires in the night where there was no sign of travelers. And in the day the hills will sparkle in the sun. I would ride to the source and find nothing there." He paused for a moment.

"It is said that the eagle and the hawk and even the grizzly are Old Ones who take new form and walk upon the earth. They lead us to new hunting grounds and give the buffalo to our people."

"You *do* have a god, a Great Spirit," the woman stated.

"Our Great Spirit is *Wakantanka*, the giver of all things. All things have life and use for our people. We sing to him and dance and are proud of all that the Great Spirit brings."

"We have a God, too," Deanne replied.

"Can your god make the bullet rise from the body of your man?" the boy asked.

"No," she replied. "There are some things that He cannot do."

"So it is with the Great Spirit. All things have a time to live and to die. People and creatures that walk the earth have few seasons. The hills and the trees and the rocks have many, many seasons. The earth and the sky live the longest. And the Old Ones. Their time is beyond what my mind can see."

The woman nodded.

"The time of your man goes away soon. He will

breathe out his spirit soon, like smoke."

Deanne looked at her husband. His breathing seemed more shallow than before. His eyelids fluttered with every breath.

"Deanne." Pat Bixby's voice came in a rusty whisper.

"I'm here, Pat," she replied. She looked into frosty eyes, saw the death there, the Beyond that had no name at such times.

"I found it, Deanne," he rasped.

"Hush, Pat. You need to save your strength."

"No. Look, Deanne. I really found it."

"Oh, Pat. You're talking out of your head." She sighed and mopped again at his brow with the wet cloth.

He moved his hand in a feeble gesture for attention. A cough rattled in his chest. He tried to push the cloth aside.

"I said for you to look." His voice was louder, more urgent this time.

"All right, Pat. Tell me where to look," she replied trying to console him.

"Up!" he answered and again gestured weakly. Deanne nodded and continued to wipe her husband's face.

"Up!" he repeated. A violent spasm of coughing ripped through him.

The woman followed the arc of the fleshy hand as it moved toward the ceiling. The soft glow of the candle barely reached the roof of the cave.

Deanne Bixby's mouth formed a small O, but emitted no sound.

Above her head, the woman saw a stripe of yellow.

The candle flickered at the vein. The stripe sparkled back.

June looked up, too, in spite of her weariness. She looked at her mother. Deanne's face looked almost radiant.

Gold. Pat Bixby had found his gold.

"See, Deanne. Told you I'd find it." The dying man's breath blew in ragged shudders. "We're rich, Deanne. Rich." Bixby raised his voice, tried to struggle up on one elbow.

"Lay yourself back down, Pat," she commanded. "You're getting too excited. Just rest now."

"Can't rest. Gotta get my pick. Gotta dig . . ." The fat man fell back onto her lap. "I found it, didn't I, Deanne? Didn't I?" His breath bubbled in his throat. Fresh blood seeped from the chest wound.

"Yes, Pat. You found it," she replied and wiped at a trickle of blood that oozed from the corner of his mouth.

"I found . . ." A long breath rushed from the man's body, then stopped. His head lolled slightly to one side. His eyes remained fixed, stared sightlessly at the vein of gold overhead.

June sobbed.

Silence filled the cave.

Pat Bixby was dead.

Chapter Seventeen

"Deanne," Gunn called softly to the sobbing woman. He watched her lean across the dead man, say her final goodbye.

"He's dead, Gunn," she said. Her face was streaked with tears, her shoulders shook with sobs. June, crying, put her arms around her father's neck.

"I'm sorry," Gunn said. He sighed. "I wish I could have gotten all of you out of here alive."

"He would've come back," Deanne said. "He wouldn't give up his dream. You could never make him do that."

"Mama?" June said, sitting up and feeling her father's chest. "Gunn, there's something here." She turned her tear-streaked face toward Gunn.

"What?" Deanne asked her daughter.

"I don't know," June said. She started to open her father's shirt. "It's a little sack of some sort."

Deanne tried to get the sack free, but she couldn't do it. "Gunn, help us with it," she pleaded.

Gunn moved over to squat beside the blood-soaked

body of Pat Bixby. Bound tightly to the dead man's neck by a rawhide strap, was a good-sized leather pouch, its smooth surface stained red. Gunn took his knife from its sheath, cut the cord from around the fleshy neck. He balanced the hide sack in his hand for a moment, feeling its weight, then he opened the pouch and poured a bit of its contents into his outstretched palm.

The firelight danced and glittered as gold dust poured out of the brown pouch.

"Whew!" Gunn whistled.

"My goodness!" Deanne exclaimed. "He did find a lot of it, didn't he?"

"That he did," Gunn replied. "At sixteen dollars to the ounce, there's enough there to get you started somewhere, keep you comfortable for a while. You wouldn't ever have to come back here again."

"Are you saying we should just walk away from this cave? We should leave this gold here?" June asked.

"That's exactly what I'm saying," Gunn said.

"So you can have it for yourself?"

"June!" Deanne scolded. "You don't mean that. I know you don't mean that."

June blinked her eyes a couple of times, and silent tears continued to flow.

"You're right," she said. "I don't mean it. I'm sorry, Mr. Gunn. I had no right to say that. It's just that . . ." She couldn't go on.

"You don't have to explain anything to me," Gunn said easily.

Deanne poured the glistening gold back into the

pouch, and June looked at it. "So," she said. "Papa finally found the gold he was always looking for."

"Yes, my dear, he finally found it," Deanne said. "You can be sure that your father died happy. For him, the search for the gold was as thrilling as the spending of it would have been. And he can rest easy knowing that he found enough for us to be comfortable if we manage it well."

The woman paused and looked up at Gunn. "And you, Gunn. There's enough here for you, too."

"No, Deanne," he replied. "I have no use for the gold. But I do want the map."

"The map? Why?" Deanne asked, surprised by his request.

"You'll see."

The tall man searched Pat Bixby's pockets and withdrew the tattered map that had been the fat man's dream. He held it out, first to Deanne and June, then to Charcoal Calf.

"Now, you have the map," Charcoal Calf said. "You think you will come back to the Paha Sapa with many more and dig out the gold. But I won't let you. Free me, Gunn. Yellow Nose told me that you defeated Stone Legs. He said also that Stone Legs gave you the red sash which made him a Strong Heart. If you are worthy to wear the sash, you must be brave enough to fight me. Cut my bonds and fight me, Gunn. Let us have a glorious fight like you did with my brother Broken Hand, and like you did with my chief, Stone Legs. Let us fight until one of us can fight no more, because one of us will be dead."

"Charcoal Calf, do you really want to kill me? Do you really want to fight to the death with me?"

"Yes!" Charcoal Calf said quickly and emphatically. "Because you are a man without a center, and a man without a center, is a man without a soul."

"Is that what you think of me?"

"Yes."

"Charcoal Calf, you think I don't understand the Paha Sapa. You believe all whites think that all things Indian are evil, and because you believe that way, you are as bad as the whites who are your enemies. I am going to talk to you now of the Paha Sapa. I am going to tell you these things, so you will know that I understand. As I speak, I want you to look into my heart, not into my mouth. I want you to hear the truth of what I say, and not just the words. Will you do this?"

"I will do this, Gunn," Charcoal Calf said. "But I do not believe that a white man can speak of the holy place."

"The Paha Sapa, what we call the Black Hills, are the center of the world," Gunn started. "They are the place of gods, holy mountains, where warriors go to speak with the Great Spirit and await visions. It is in the Black Hills where those-who-have-gone-before and those-yet-to-come meet and give wisdom to those who are here now. There is a treaty which says the white man has given the Black Hills to the Sioux. But the Sioux laugh at the vanity of the white man who says such a thing. The Black Hills did not belong to the white man to give to the Sioux. The Black HIlls have been here as long as the earth itself, and when the Great Spirit allows someone to be born, the great spirit gives him the earth, as he gives him air to breathe and water to drink."

Gunn looked at the two women, then at Charcoal Calf. Charcoal Calf appeared to be stunned by the wisdom of Gunn's words. Gunn went on.

"Now, there has been gold discovered in the Paha Sapa. The white men want the gold, and to get it, they will come to the Black Hills and dig it out any way they can. They will have no respect for the spirits who live in the hills and no honor for the Sioux who say the hills are sacred to them. When they hear of the gold, they know only greed, and greed and respect cannot live in the same house. If this goes on, something will happen."

"What?" Deanne asked. "What will happen?"

"I'm afraid there's going to be a big battle," Gunn said. "Soldiers against Indians. There will be many killed on both sides, and crying in the tipis and in the white men's houses back east."

"You are speaking of the battle which will happen in the month of making fat, at the place called Greasy Grass. The soldiers will be defeated," Charcoal Calf put in quickly. "I was told this in a vision. There will be a great victory for the Lakota."

"If this is true, it is a bad thing for the Indian," Gunn said.

"How can it be a bad thing for the Indian if the Indian knows a great victory?" Charcoal Calf wanted to know.

"Because then the white chiefs will wake from their sleep," Gunn warned. "And they will send more soldiers than there are blades of grass. They will move across the plains like a plague of locusts, destroying everyone and everything in their path. They will kill the Brules, the Minneconjou, the Cheyenne, the Mandan, the Apache, the Kiowa, the Navajo, even the Crow who has always been friends to the white man. If this happens, all the plains Indians will go the way of the Mohegan."

"The Mohegan?" Charcoal Calf asked. "What is Mohegan?"

"The Mohegans were once mighty warriors, like the Sioux. They are no more. The white men killed them all."

Charcoal Calf was silent for a long moment.

"I am not proud of my race for doing this," Gunn said. "And I would not want to see that happen to the Brules."

"I have looked into your heart as you spoke," Charcoal Calf said.

"And, what have you seen?"

"I have seen the truth."

"I am glad," Gunn said. "Now, we're going to put an end to the trouble on the Holy Road." He was still holding the map, and he held the stained and ragged paper to the fire. The flames licked at the edge of the paper, then caught the map in its blaze. The brown ring of fire crept up the document toward Gunn's hand, blackened the drawing, ate at the marks. Not until the map was almost entirely consumed, did

Gunn release the remaining corner and let it drop into the leaping fire.

The two women, mesmerized, looked on in mute fascination.

The Indian boy watched the flames burn the last corner of the evil paper. When the last ash had disintegrated, Gunn turned to the brave. "This map will cause no more trouble for the Indian people in the sacred Black Hills," he said.

The boy nodded his approval.

"Now, Charcoal Calf. Do you still want to fight me to the death? Do you still think that I am your enemy?"

Charcoal Calf shook his head. "No," he said. "I no longer want to kill you."

"I'm going to cut your bindings, Charcoal Calf, and let you return to your people." Gunn moved toward the boy, the Mexican knife in his hand. "When you see them, tell them there are wise men who are white and wise men who are red. If the wise men will speak, brave men will not have to die."

"I will tell them this," Charcoal Calf promised.

Before Gunn could cut the cords, a horse nickered, stamped somewhere outside.

Gunn swung his head around to seek the cause of the restless horse.

"*Aheeeee!*" came a bloodcurdling cry from the brush outside the cave.

"It is the crazy one," Charcoal Calf whispered. "He is called Walks With Ghosts. He was with us during the fighting, but he was shot. I thought he was dead."

Gunn eased his tall frame closer to the opening, laid his body flat against the stone wall.

"Stay back," he whispered to the women.

There was movement a few yards beyond the brush.

Esquire whinnied.

Gunn whistled low. The horse jerked its head up, perked its ears.

"Boy," the man called quietly to the nervous animal.

The loosely-tied horse flicked his head, pulled the reins from their knot on the bush. The big sorrel ambled cautiously toward its master.

Gingerly, Gunn shifted his position as the horse approached. He stepped out, swung one boot into the stirrup and grabbed a hand hold on the saddle horn. He crouched, clung to the side of the horse.

The big Walker held the off-sided weight and responded to Gunn's clucking tongue. The animal started down the slope with its rider clinging to the side like a Comanche brave.

He laid the reins on Esquire's neck and turned him. He rode in a semi-circle, slowly.

He saw nothing.

Then a flicker, a shadow within a shadow, already gone by the time he looked. A whisper, growing louder and louder, hissed toward him, whirring like a thrown stick. An object hurtled toward him.

A lasso? No.

A snake!

The rattler fell into the bush beyond him, slithered away, rattling in angry challenge.

The snake accomplished its purpose for the man who threw it, though, because Esquire bolted at the moving snake, then sunfished quickly to rid himself of his rider's weight.

Gunn grabbed for a hold, but he wasn't seated, and there was nothing to keep him on the horse. He felt the sickening sensation of empty space beneath him as the horse threw him from his precarious position on the stirrup.

The big man hit the ground with a bone-rattling thud, felt his gut drive up into his chest. He sprawled on the ground, waited to regain his wind.

He realized that he was in the open then, and he scooted toward a nearby bush, just as a bullet plowed a furrow where he had been an instant before. The explosion of the Indian's rifle echoed across the open gully. Gunn slipped in farther, until he was completely out of sight, even to someone standing right by the bush. Let the Indian come look for him if he wanted him. Gunn was ready.

Wait, he thought. Like trying to catch a frisky horse. Lie still and wait. This crazy one would get curious and come up to him, find him. He pulled the hammer back on his pistol, cocking it slowly, turning the cylinder until a fresh load was under the hammer, ready for firing. Then he waited.

The sun climbed higher, the temperature grew hotter. Still, he waited.

A fly buzzed around Gunn's face, landed on his nose and dabbled in the sweat for a brief moment. A muscle throbbed in his cheek. The fly buzzed for a moment, flew away.

A lizard came scurrying by, obviously frightened by something. By what? Gunn wondered. The sniper had to be prowling around, looking, poking under the bushes and behind the rocks, trying to find Gunn.

Gunn waited.

A branch cracked to the right a few yards down the slope.

Gunn rolled his eyes, peered in the direction of the sound. A nerve twitched somewhere along his spine.

A small pebble clinked, the sound closer.

The swish of cloth moved close to him. The smell of bear grease and tanned hide were missing. Gunn thought that unusual, but he had no time to contemplate it. He was suddenly surprised at the sight of a man standing right by his bush. The Indian was so close, Gunn could see the toes of the man's moccasins.

The lift of a hide-covered heel was all the warning Gunn needed.

"*Aheee!*" the lurking man cried again. The man fired his rifle into the bush, just as Gunn rolled away. Gunn gained his feet then swung his gun toward the man who had attacked him. This was his first glimpse of the crazy one Charcoal Calf called Walks With Ghosts.

Gunn had never seen such a wild looking man in his life. His hair was matted, his clothes soiled and tattered, his words jibberish as he hopped from one moccasined foot to the other in some sort of dancing frenzy. The most amazing thing about him though, was the fact that he wasn't an Indian. His face was covered with months of dirt, and a matted, filthy beard. Walks With Ghosts was a white man.

The old man cocked his rifle, levering a shell into the chamber. As yet, he hadn't raised it. He chanted, something low and unintelligible.

"Look, old man," Gunn reasoned. "There's something wrong with you. You've been out here too long. Let me take you back. I don't want to hurt you."

The tattered man continued his strange-sounding chant.

"I'm warning you. Step back and I won't hurt you!"

The man raised his rifle to his shoulder.

"No!" Gunn said. "Don't do it! Don't make me kill you!"

Gunn did not want to kill this man. It went against everything he believed in, this killing of lesser things, of helpless things. But this one wasn't helpless. Crazy as a loon, maybe, but dangerous as a rattler in a bread box. There was fire in the old man's blue eyes, determination in his voice, in his infernal chant.

The two stood there, eyeing each other warily, the ragged man breathing through his nose like a snorting bull. Gunn was watching the man's trigger finger. The moment it started to twitch, he would shoot.

"Gunn!" Deanne's voice called. She suddenly appeared on the hillside.

"No!" Gunn shouted. "No, go back!"

Gunn's eye flickered with the distraction and the old man fired. Perhaps it was because he expected the man to fire, that Gunn threw himself to the ground at almost the same instant. The bullet whizzed by, so close to his ear that he could hear it whip as it snapped by. He landed on the ground and rolled. The action prevented him from being shot, but it also caused him to drop his pistol. He started to reach for it, but the man cocked his rifle again, and aimed right at Gunn. It would be impossible for him to miss again.

"Gunn, are you all right?" Deanne called. She was nearly on them now.

"Stay back, Deanne," Gunn called.

The wild man's eyes flickered toward Deanne, and that was just the opening Gunn was looking for. He rolled quickly, grabbed his pistol, rolled again and this time fired. His bullet slammed into the wild man's chest. The wild man dropped his rifle, then stood there, swaying back and forth. Gunn leaped to his feet. "Stay back, Deanne," he called again.

"Deanne?" the wild man said. He sank to his knees, the blood gushing down his front. "Deanne?" This time there was a strange, almost plaintive note to his call. He fell face down among the rocks.

Gunn stared at the back of the fallen man, puzzled by the dead man's last word.

"It's over," Gunn said to the woman who had been a horrified witness to the whole scene. He rolled the dead man onto his back and looked down at him. Cautiously, Deanne came the rest of the way down the hill. She stood there and looked into the dead man's face.

"Oh, my God. No," she said, sobbing at the sight

of the filthy body. "No," she repeated and kneeled beside the lifeless form.

"Oh, Gunn. This is terrible." Her wail broke through the shadows of the coming night.

Charcoal Calf came down the hill and stood with June Bixby, as she looked on. They were as puzzled by Deanne's strange behavior as Gunn.

"Mama?" June questioned. "Mama, what is it? What's wrong?"

"Deanne," Gunn whispered and gripped the woman's arms, pulled her over to the dead man's side.

The suffering woman allowed herself to be lifted to her feet, but she continued to look down at the body of the man Gunn had just killed.

"Mama?" June asked again. "Who is that man?"

"It's Jack," she whispered through her tears. "Pat's brother, Jack Bixby."

"Well, I'll be damned," said Gunn.

THE NEWEST ADVENTURES AND ESCAPADES OF BOLT
by Cort Martin

#11: THE LAST BORDELLO (1224, $2.25)
A working girl in Angel's camp doesn't stand a chance—unless Jared Bolt takes up arms to bring a little peace to the town . . . and discovers that the trouble is caused by a woman who used to do the same!

#12: THE HANGTOWN HARLOTS (1274, $2.25)
When the miners come to town, the local girls are used to having wild parties, but events are turning ugly . . . and murderous. Jared Bolt knows the trade of tricking better than anyone, though, and is always the first to come to a lady in need . . .

#13: MONTANA MISTRESS (1316, $2.25)
Roland Cameron owns the local bank, the sheriff, and the town—and he thinks he owns the sensuous saloon singer, Charity, as well. But the moment Bolt and Charity eye each other there's fire—especially gunfire!

#14: VIRGINIA CITY VIRGIN (1360, $2.25)
When Katie's bawdy house holds a high stakes raffle, Bolt figures to take a chance. It's winner take all—and the prize is a budding nineteen year old virgin! But there's a passle of gun-toting folks who'd rather see Bolt in a coffin than in the virgin's bed!

#15: BORDELLO BACKSHOOTER (1411, $2.25)
Nobody has ever seen the face of curvaceous Cherry Bonner, the mysterious madam of the bawdiest bordello in Cheyenne. When Bolt keeps a pimp with big ideas and a terrible temper from having his way with Cherry, gunfire flares and a gambling man would bet on murder: Bolt's!

#16: HARDCASE HUSSY (1513, $2.25)
Traveling to set up his next bordello, Bolt is surrounded by six prime ladies of the evening. But just as Bolt is about to explore this lovely terrain, their stagecoach is ambushed by the murdering Beeler gang, bucking to be in Bolt's position!

Available wherever paperbacks are sold, or order direct from the Publisher. Send cover price plus 50¢ per copy for mailing and handling to Zebra Books, Dept. 1852, 475 Park Avenue South, New York, N.Y. 10016. DO NOT SEND CASH.